The Story of
SHERLOCK HOLMES
The Famous Detective

Sherlock Holmes and his helpful friend Dr. John Watson are fictional characters created by British writer Sir Arthur Conan Doyle. Doyle published his first novel about the pair, *A Study in Scarlet*, in 1887, and it became very successful. Doyle went on to write fifty-six short stories, as well as three more novels about Holmes's adventures—*The Sign of Four* (1890), *The Hound of the Baskervilles* (1902), and *The Valley of Fear* (1915).

Sherlock Holmes and Dr. Watson have become some of the most famous book characters of all time. Holmes spent most of his time solving mysteries, but he also had a wide array of hobbies, such as playing the violin, boxing, and sword fighting. Watson, a retired army doctor, met Holmes through a mutual friend when Holmes was looking for a roommate. Watson lived with Holmes for several years at 221B Baker Street before marrying and moving out. However, after his marriage, Watson continued to assist Holmes with his cases.

The original versions of the Sherlock Holmes stories are still printed, and many have been made into movies and television shows. Readers continue to be impressed by Holmes's detective methods of observation and scientific reason.

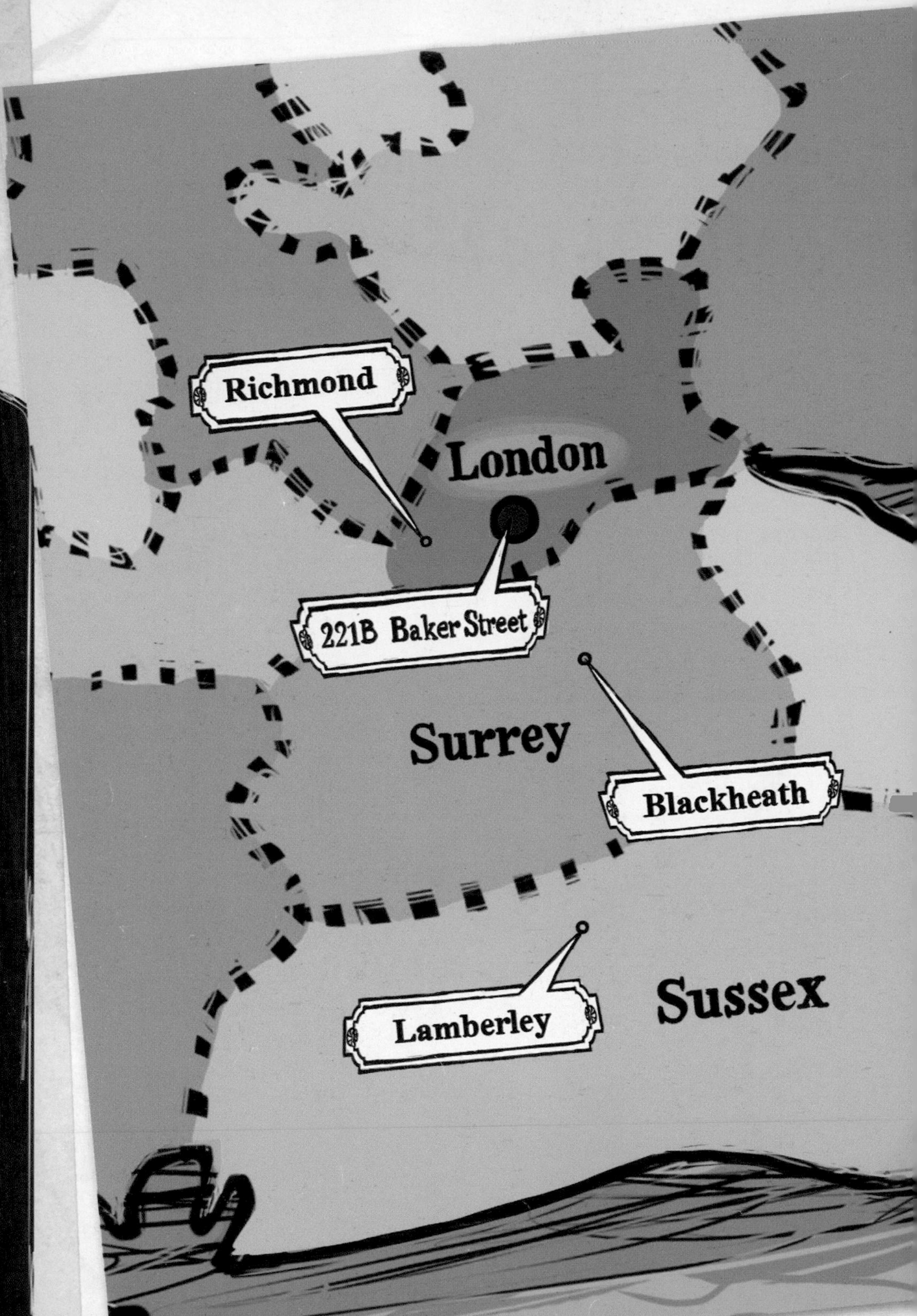
Richmond
London
221B Baker Street
Surrey
Blackheath
Sussex
Lamberley

6

ON the CASE with HOLMES and WATSON

SHERLOCK HOLMES

and the Adventure of the Sussex Vampire

Based on the stories of
Sir Arthur Conan Doyle

Adapted by Murray Shaw and M. J. Cosson
Illustrated by Sophie Rohrbach

GRAPHIC UNIVERSE™ • MINNEAPOLIS • NEW YORK • LONDON

Grateful acknowledgment to Dame Jean Conan Doyle for permission to use the
Sherlock Holmes characters created by Sir Arthur Conan Doyle

Text copyright © 2011 by Murray Shaw
Illustrations © 2011 by Lerner Publishing Group, Inc.

Graphic Universe™ is a trademark of Lerner Publishing Group, Inc.

Graphic Universe™
A division of Lerner Publishing Group, Inc.
241 First Avenue North
Minneapolis, MN 55401 U.S.A.

Website address: www.lernerbooks.com

Library of Congress Cataloging-in-Publication Data

Shaw, Murray.
    #6 Sherlock Holmes and the adventure of the Sussex vampire / adapted
by Murray Shaw and M.J. Cosson ; illustrated by Sophie Rohrbach ; from the
original stories by Sir Arthur Conan Doyle.
        p.   cm. — (On the case with Holmes and Watson)
    Summary: Retold in graphic novel form, Sherlock Holmes investigates a
report of a young wife sucking the blood from her infant son. Includes a
section explaining Holmes's reasoning and the clues he used to solve the
mystery.
    ISBN: 978-0-7613-6187-9 (lib. bdg. : alk. paper)
    I. Graphic novels. (I. Graphic novels. 2. Doyle, Arthur Conan, Sir,
1859–1930. Adventure of the Sussex vampire—Adaptations. 3. Mystery and
detective stories.) I. Cosson, M. J. II. Rohrbach, Sophie, ill. III. Doyle,
Arthur Conan, Sir, 1859–1930. Adventure of the Sussex vampire. IV. Title.
V. Title: Adventure of the Sussex vampire.
    PZ7.7.S46Shs 2011
    741.5'973—dc22   2009051762 9

Manufactured in the United States of America
2—BC—2/1/11

Character List

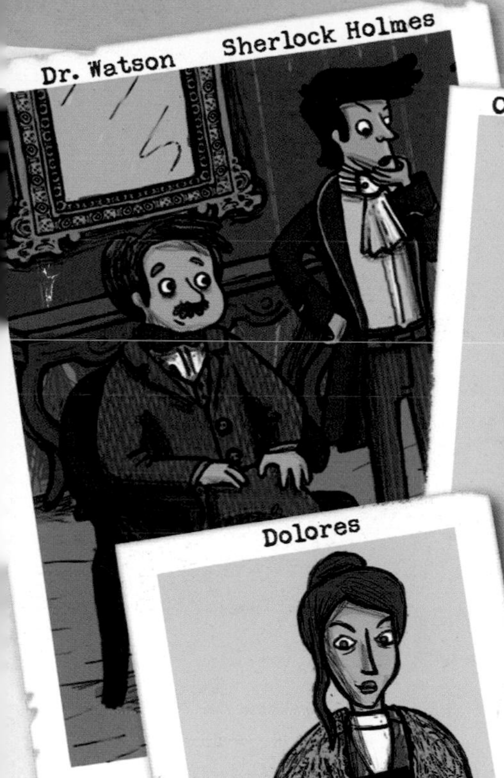
Dr. Watson
Sherlock Holmes

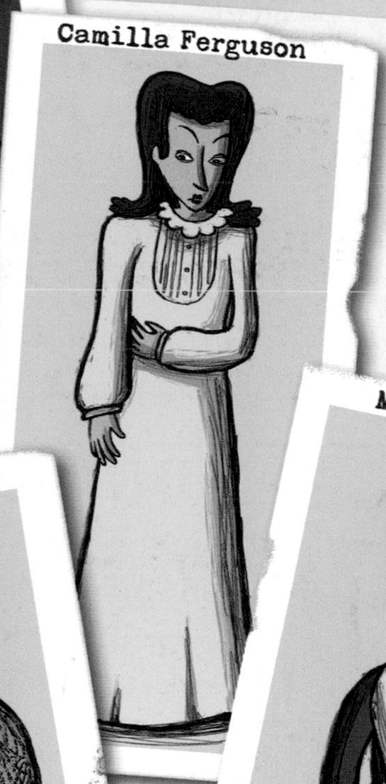
Camilla Ferguson

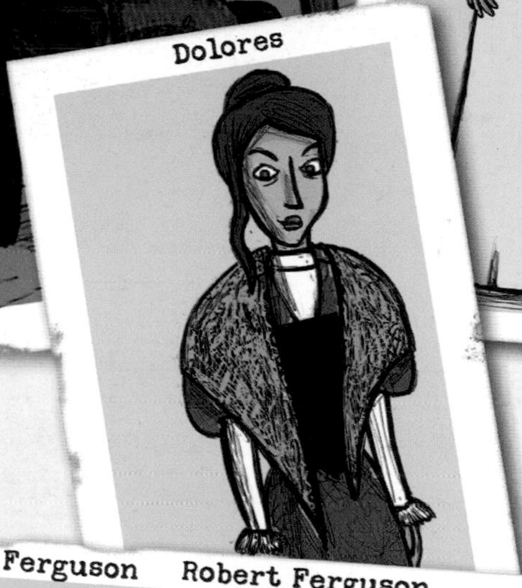
Dolores

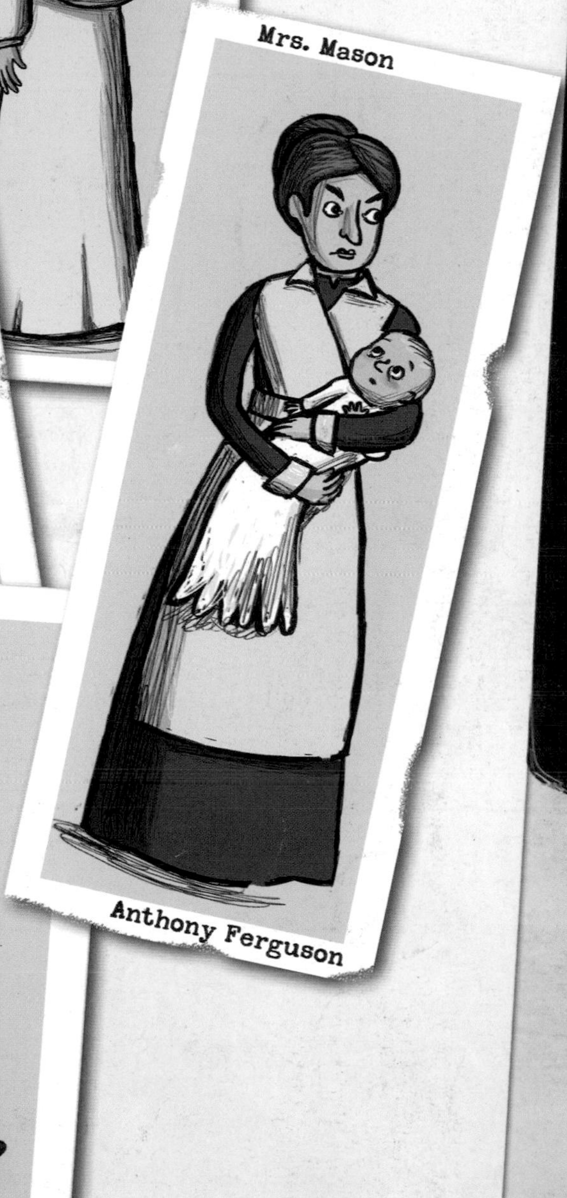
Mrs. Mason
Anthony Ferguson

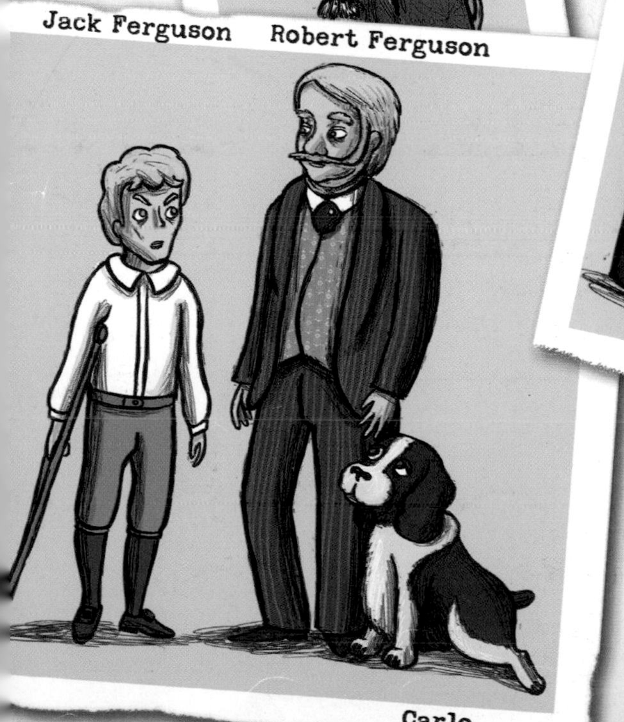
Jack Ferguson
Robert Ferguson
Carlo

From the Desk of John H. Watson, M.D.

My name is Dr. John H. Watson. For several years, I have been assisting my friend, Sherlock Holmes, in solving mysteries throughout the bustling city of London and beyond. Holmes is a peculiar man—always questioning and reasoning his way through various problems. But when I first met him in 1878, I was immediately intrigued by his oddities.

Holmes has always been more daring than I, and his logical deduction never ceases to amaze me. I have begun writing down all of the adventures I have with Holmes. This is one of those stories.

Sincerely,

Dr. Watson

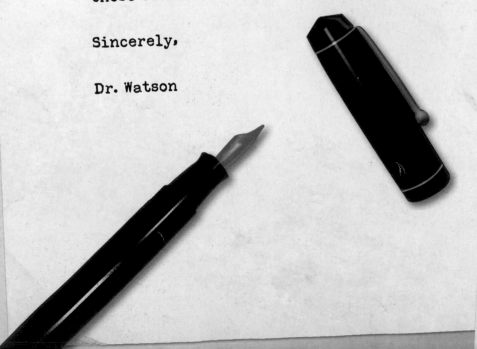

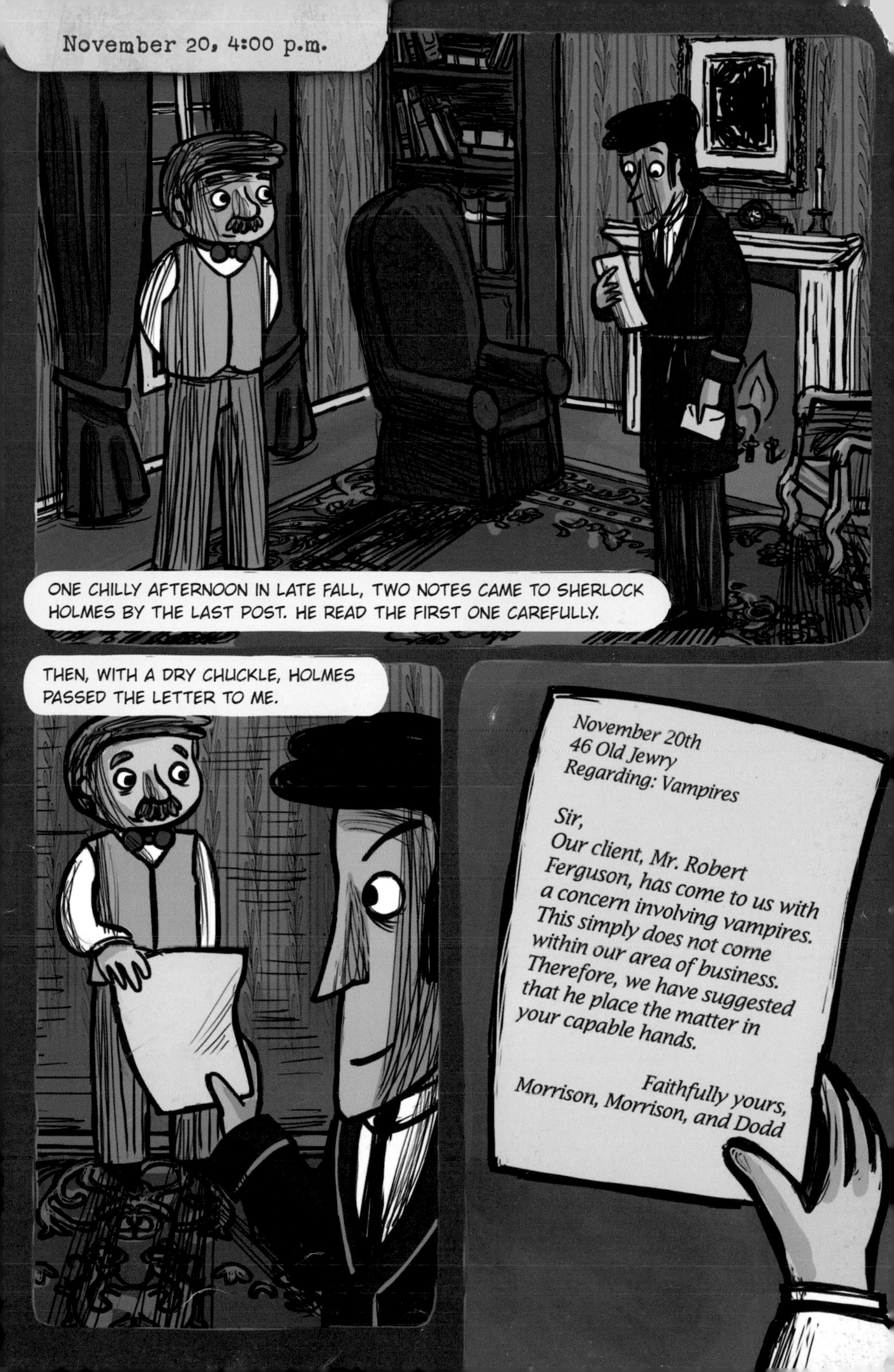
November 20, 4:00 p.m.
ONE CHILLY AFTERNOON IN LATE FALL, TWO NOTES CAME TO SHERLOCK HOLMES BY THE LAST POST. HE READ THE FIRST ONE CAREFULLY.
THEN, WITH A DRY CHUCKLE, HOLMES PASSED THE LETTER TO ME.
November 20th
46 Old Jewry
Regarding: Vampires
Sir,
Our client, Mr. Robert Ferguson, has come to us with a concern involving vampires. This simply does not come within our area of business. Therefore, we have suggested that he place the matter in your capable hands.
Faithfully yours,
Morrison, Morrison, and Dodd

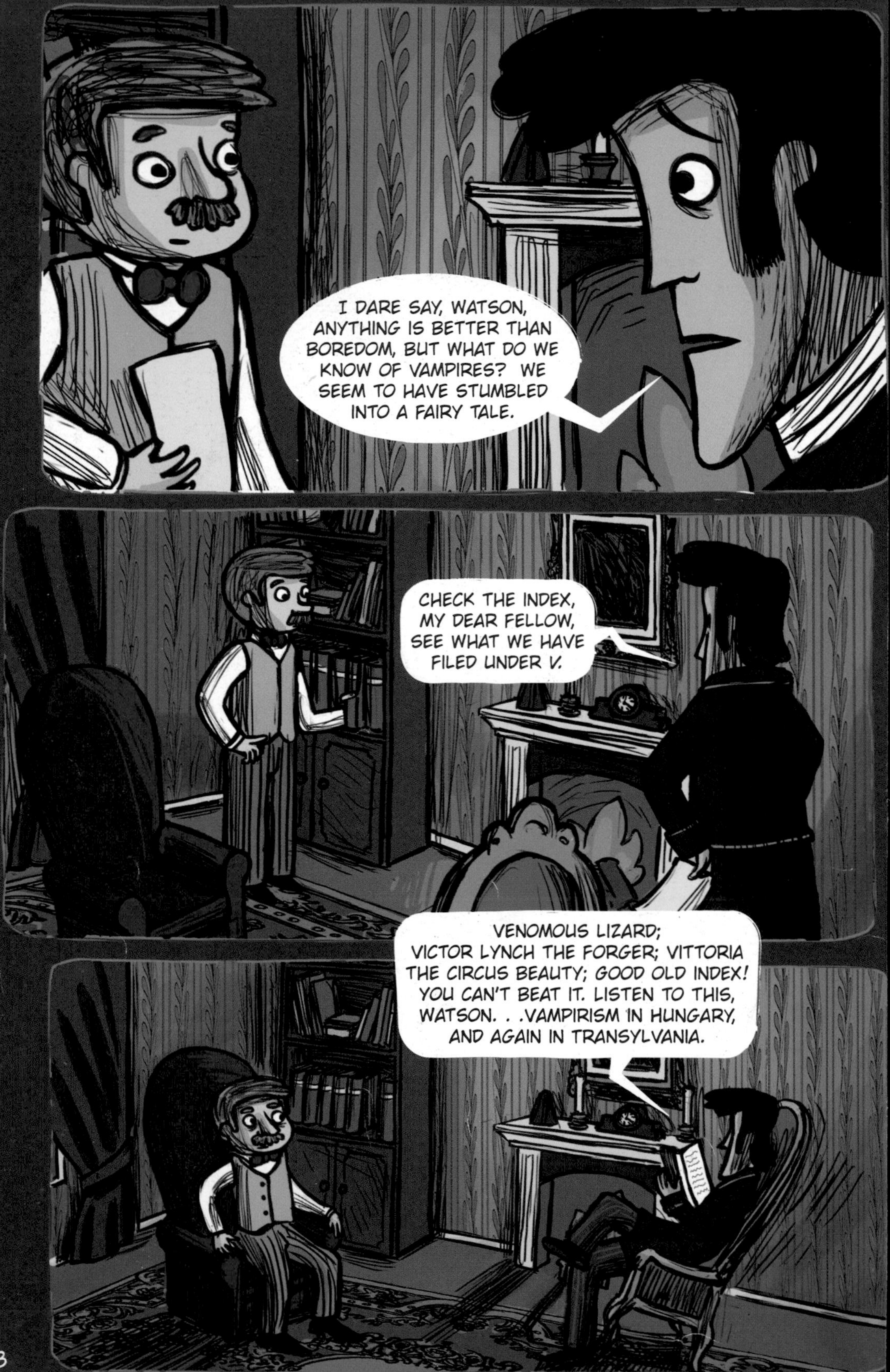
I DARE SAY, WATSON, ANYTHING IS BETTER THAN BOREDOM, BUT WHAT DO WE KNOW OF VAMPIRES? WE SEEM TO HAVE STUMBLED INTO A FAIRY TALE.
CHECK THE INDEX, MY DEAR FELLOW, SEE WHAT WE HAVE FILED UNDER V.
VENOMOUS LIZARD; VICTOR LYNCH THE FORGER; VITTORIA THE CIRCUS BEAUTY; GOOD OLD INDEX! YOU CAN'T BEAT IT. LISTEN TO THIS, WATSON. . .VAMPIRISM IN HUNGARY, AND AGAIN IN TRANSYLVANIA.

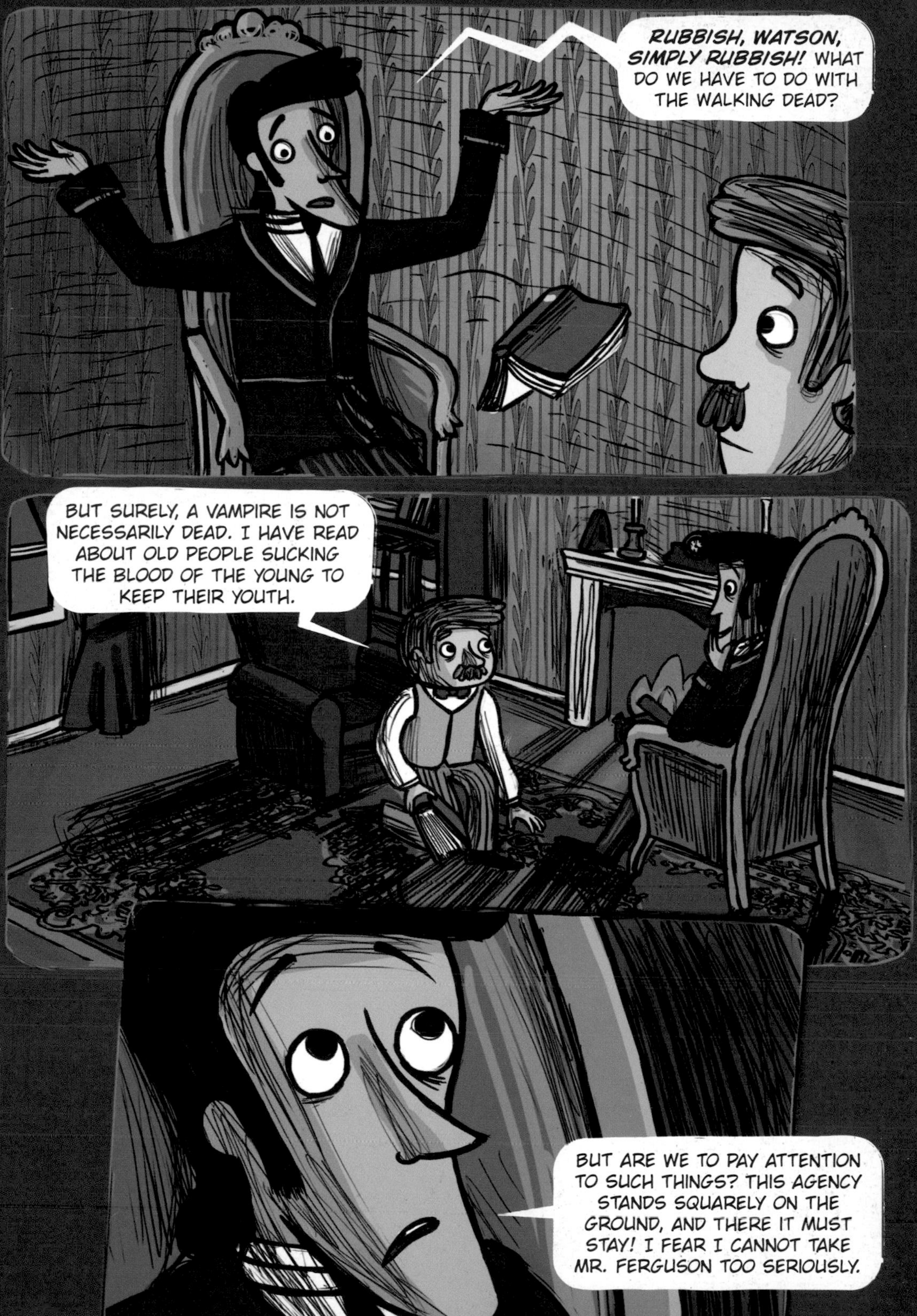
RUBBISH, WATSON, SIMPLY RUBBISH! WHAT DO WE HAVE TO DO WITH THE WALKING DEAD?
BUT SURELY, A VAMPIRE IS NOT NECESSARILY DEAD. I HAVE READ ABOUT OLD PEOPLE SUCKING THE BLOOD OF THE YOUNG TO KEEP THEIR YOUTH.
BUT ARE WE TO PAY ATTENTION TO SUCH THINGS? THIS AGENCY STANDS SQUARELY ON THE GROUND, AND THERE IT MUST STAY! I FEAR I CANNOT TAKE MR. FERGUSON TOO SERIOUSLY.

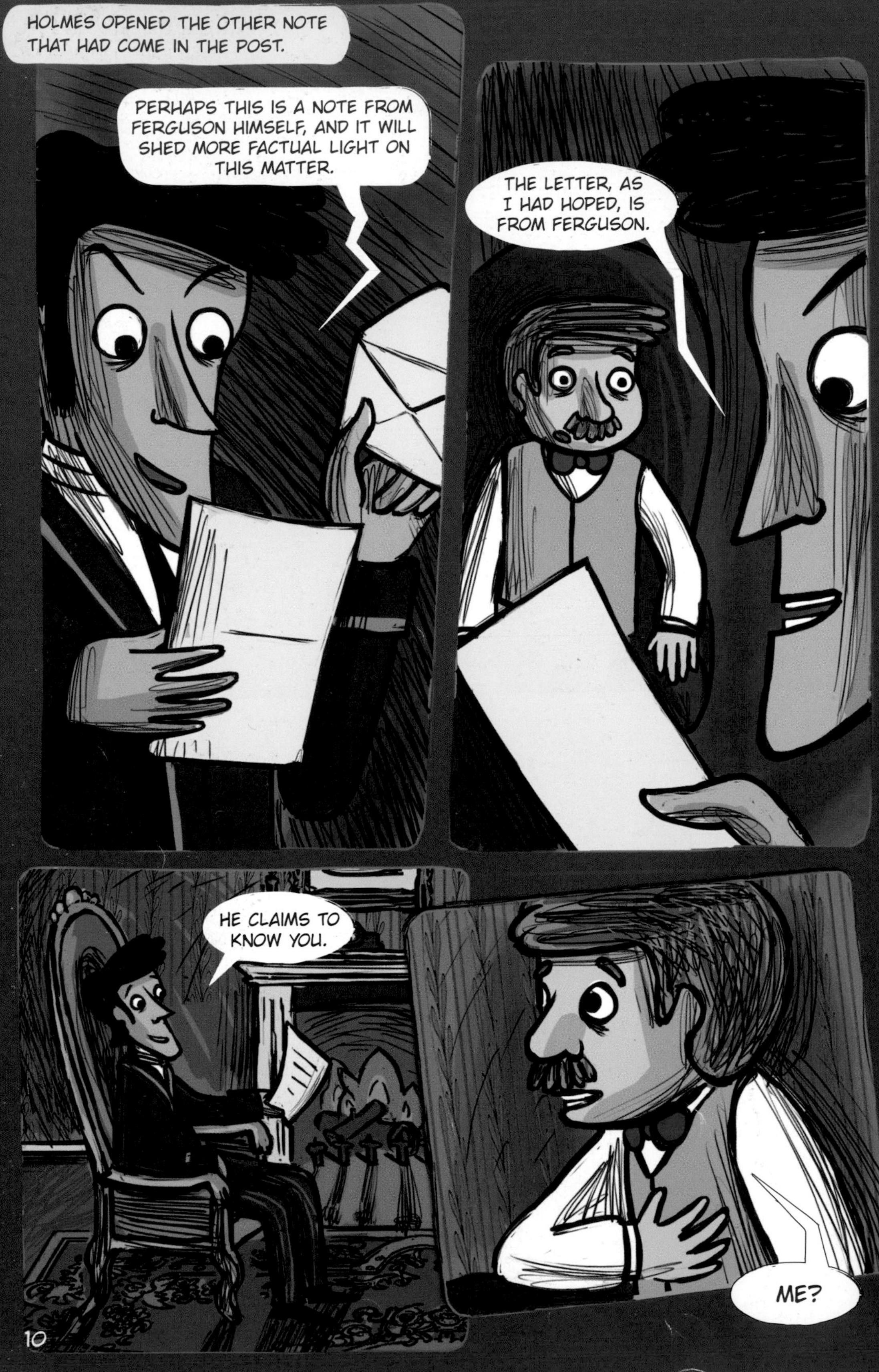
HOLMES OPENED THE OTHER NOTE THAT HAD COME IN THE POST.
PERHAPS THIS IS A NOTE FROM FERGUSON HIMSELF, AND IT WILL SHED MORE FACTUAL LIGHT ON THIS MATTER.
THE LETTER, AS I HAD HOPED, IS FROM FERGUSON.
HE CLAIMS TO KNOW YOU.
ME?

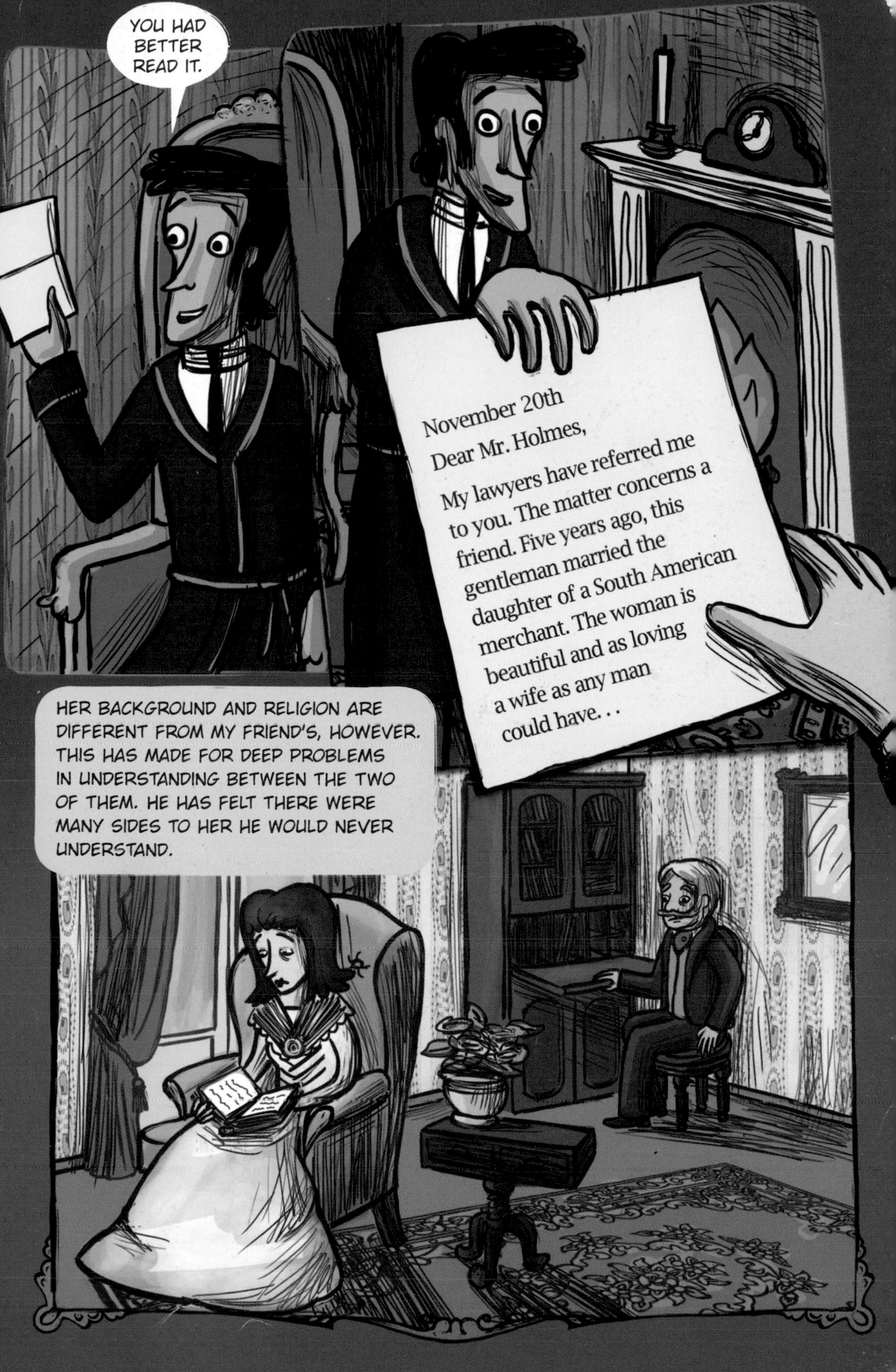
YOU HAD BETTER READ IT.
November 20th
Dear Mr. Holmes,
My lawyers have referred me to you. The matter concerns a friend. Five years ago, this gentleman married the daughter of a South American merchant. The woman is beautiful and as loving a wife as any man could have. . .
HER BACKGROUND AND RELIGION ARE DIFFERENT FROM MY FRIEND'S, HOWEVER. THIS HAS MADE FOR DEEP PROBLEMS IN UNDERSTANDING BETWEEN THE TWO OF THEM. HE HAS FELT THERE WERE MANY SIDES TO HER HE WOULD NEVER UNDERSTAND.

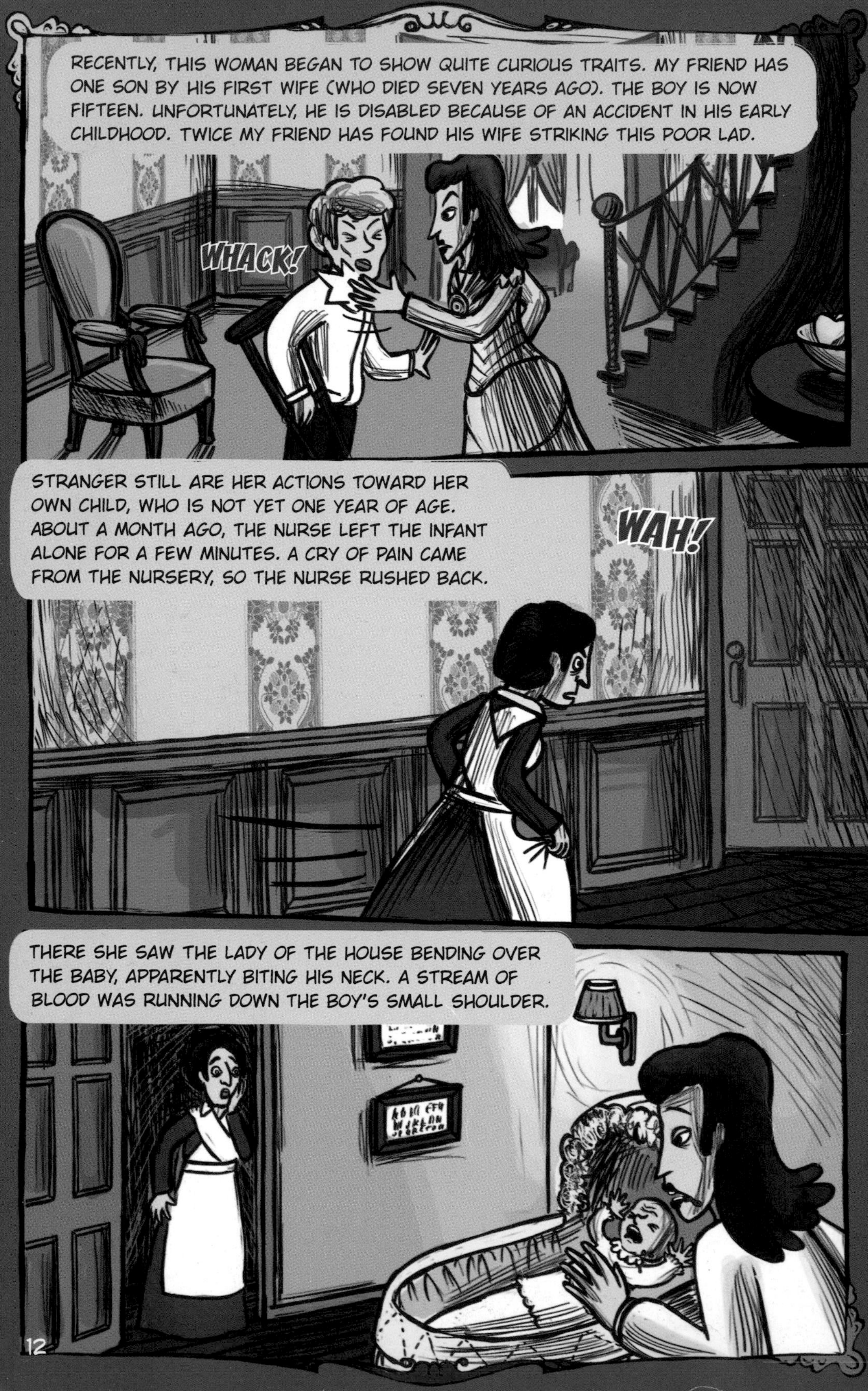
RECENTLY, THIS WOMAN BEGAN TO SHOW QUITE CURIOUS TRAITS. MY FRIEND HAS ONE SON BY HIS FIRST WIFE (WHO DIED SEVEN YEARS AGO). THE BOY IS NOW FIFTEEN. UNFORTUNATELY, HE IS DISABLED BECAUSE OF AN ACCIDENT IN HIS EARLY CHILDHOOD. TWICE MY FRIEND HAS FOUND HIS WIFE STRIKING THIS POOR LAD.
WHACK!
STRANGER STILL ARE HER ACTIONS TOWARD HER OWN CHILD, WHO IS NOT YET ONE YEAR OF AGE. ABOUT A MONTH AGO, THE NURSE LEFT THE INFANT ALONE FOR A FEW MINUTES. A CRY OF PAIN CAME FROM THE NURSERY, SO THE NURSE RUSHED BACK.
WAH!
THERE SHE SAW THE LADY OF THE HOUSE BENDING OVER THE BABY, APPARENTLY BITING HIS NECK. A STREAM OF BLOOD WAS RUNNING DOWN THE BOY'S SMALL SHOULDER.

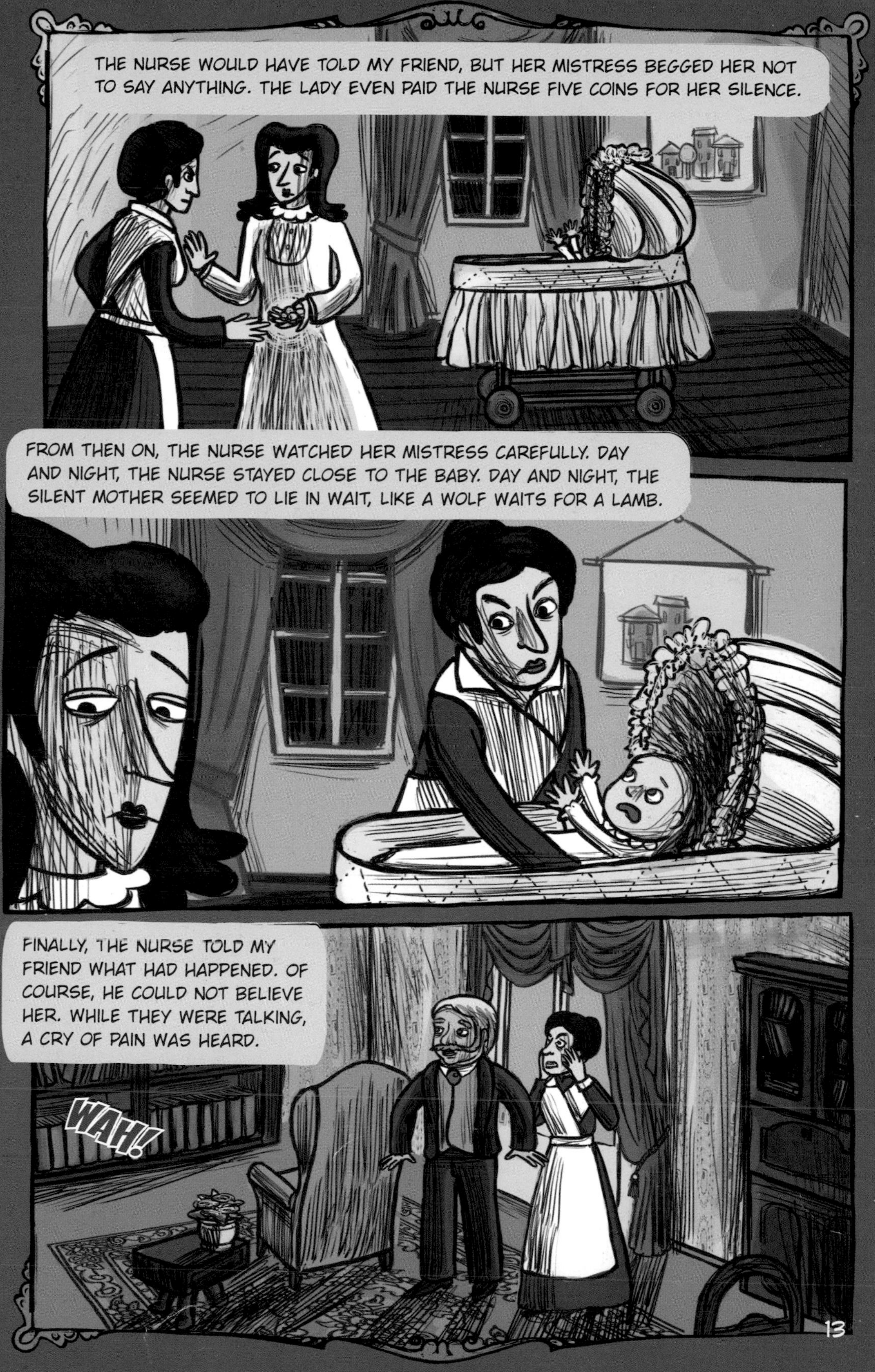
THE NURSE WOULD HAVE TOLD MY FRIEND, BUT HER MISTRESS BEGGED HER NOT TO SAY ANYTHING. THE LADY EVEN PAID THE NURSE FIVE COINS FOR HER SILENCE.
FROM THEN ON, THE NURSE WATCHED HER MISTRESS CAREFULLY. DAY AND NIGHT, THE NURSE STAYED CLOSE TO THE BABY. DAY AND NIGHT, THE SILENT MOTHER SEEMED TO LIE IN WAIT, LIKE A WOLF WAITS FOR A LAMB.
FINALLY, THE NURSE TOLD MY FRIEND WHAT HAD HAPPENED. OF COURSE, HE COULD NOT BELIEVE HER. WHILE THEY WERE TALKING, A CRY OF PAIN WAS HEARD.
WAH!

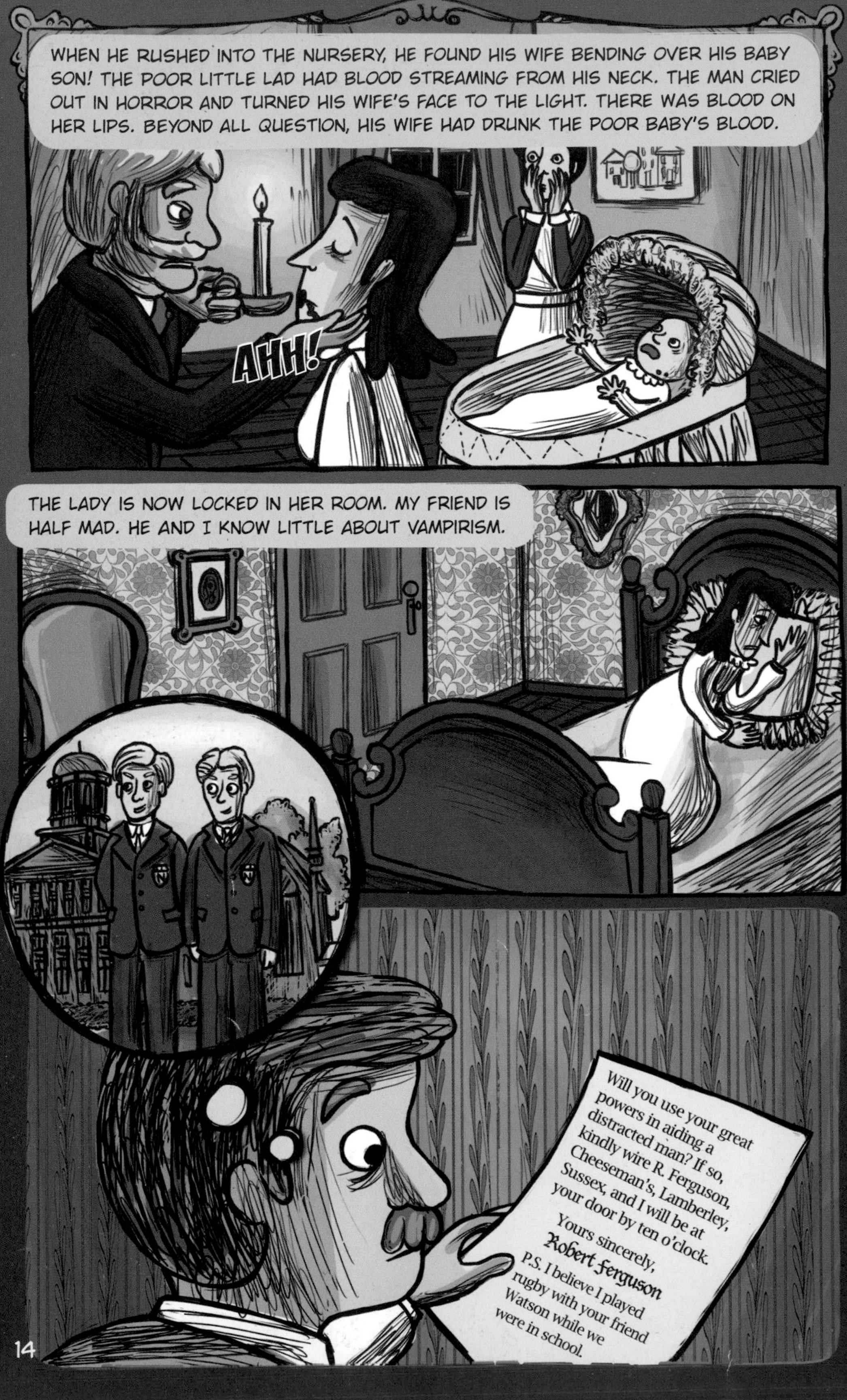
WHEN HE RUSHED INTO THE NURSERY, HE FOUND HIS WIFE BENDING OVER HIS BABY SON! THE POOR LITTLE LAD HAD BLOOD STREAMING FROM HIS NECK. THE MAN CRIED OUT IN HORROR AND TURNED HIS WIFE'S FACE TO THE LIGHT. THERE WAS BLOOD ON HER LIPS. BEYOND ALL QUESTION, HIS WIFE HAD DRUNK THE POOR BABY'S BLOOD.
AHH!
THE LADY IS NOW LOCKED IN HER ROOM. MY FRIEND IS HALF MAD. HE AND I KNOW LITTLE ABOUT VAMPIRISM.
Will you use your great powers in aiding a distracted man? If so, kindly wire R. Ferguson, Cheeseman's, Lamberley, Sussex, and I will be at your door by ten o'clock.
Yours sincerely,
Robert Ferguson
P.S. I believe I played rugby with your friend Watson while we were in school.

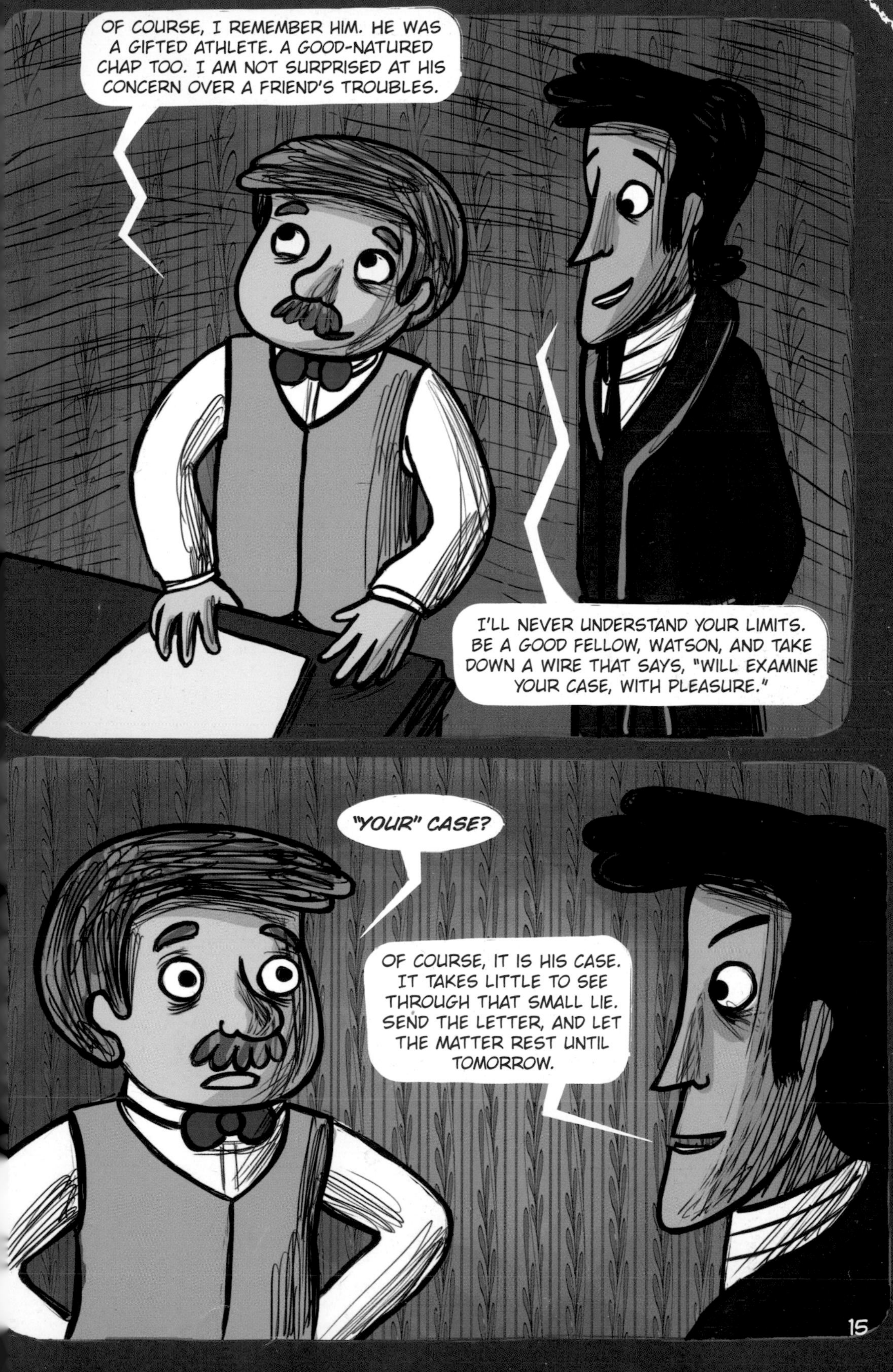
OF COURSE, I REMEMBER HIM. HE WAS A GIFTED ATHLETE. A GOOD-NATURED CHAP TOO. I AM NOT SURPRISED AT HIS CONCERN OVER A FRIEND'S TROUBLES.
I'LL NEVER UNDERSTAND YOUR LIMITS. BE A GOOD FELLOW, WATSON, AND TAKE DOWN A WIRE THAT SAYS, "WILL EXAMINE YOUR CASE, WITH PLEASURE."
"YOUR" CASE?
OF COURSE, IT IS HIS CASE. IT TAKES LITTLE TO SEE THROUGH THAT SMALL LIE. SEND THE LETTER, AND LET THE MATTER REST UNTIL TOMORROW.

November 21, 10:00 a.m.

Promptly at ten o'clock the next morning, Robert Ferguson strode into the room. This was hardly the great athlete he had been during school. His blond hair was scanty, his shoulders had bowed, and his muscular frame had grown flabby. I feared that he was seeing the same changes in me.

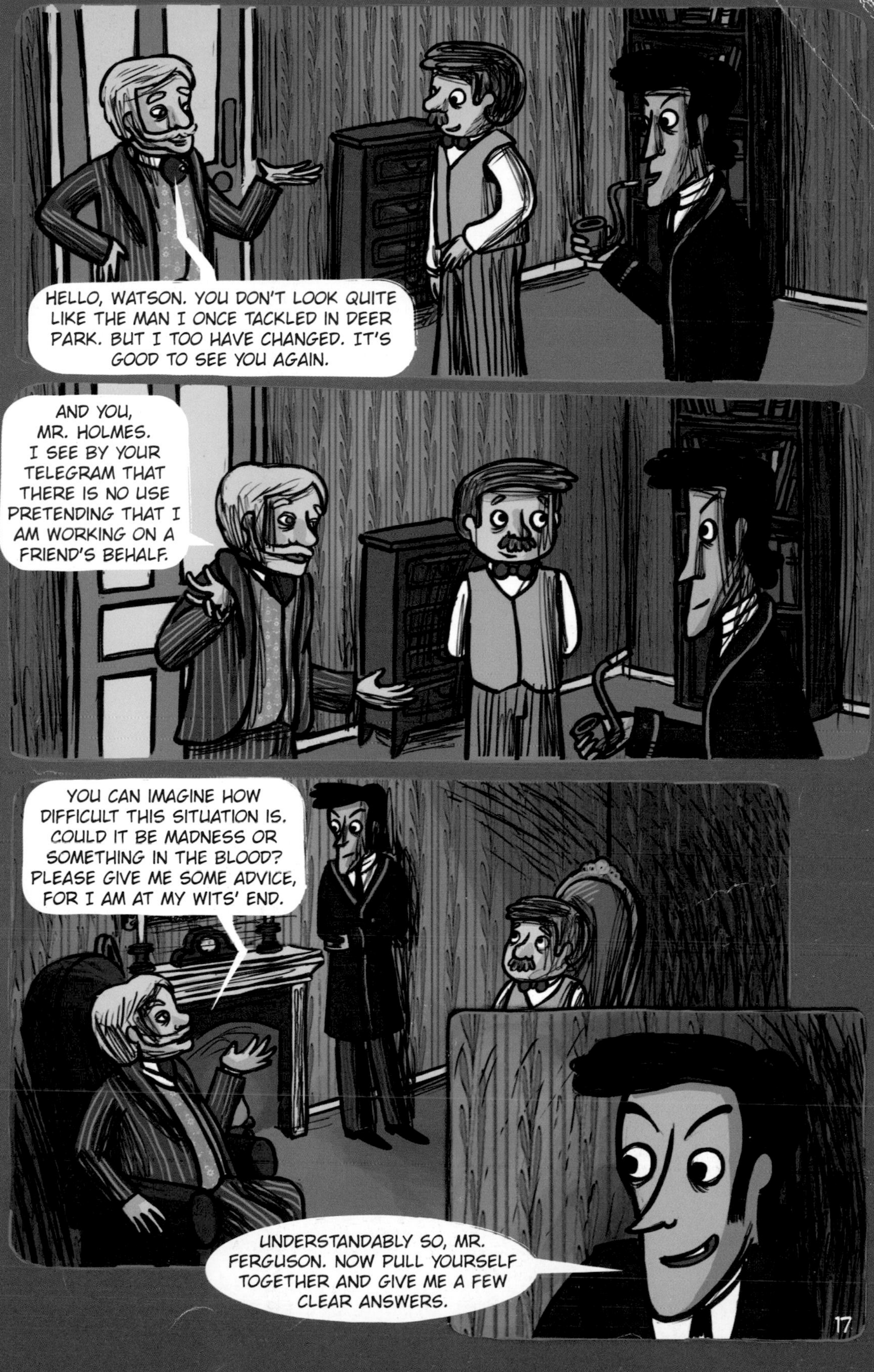
HELLO, WATSON. YOU DON'T LOOK QUITE LIKE THE MAN I ONCE TACKLED IN DEER PARK. BUT I TOO HAVE CHANGED. IT'S GOOD TO SEE YOU AGAIN.
AND YOU, MR. HOLMES. I SEE BY YOUR TELEGRAM THAT THERE IS NO USE PRETENDING THAT I AM WORKING ON A FRIEND'S BEHALF.
YOU CAN IMAGINE HOW DIFFICULT THIS SITUATION IS. COULD IT BE MADNESS OR SOMETHING IN THE BLOOD? PLEASE GIVE ME SOME ADVICE, FOR I AM AT MY WITS' END.
UNDERSTANDABLY SO, MR. FERGUSON. NOW PULL YOURSELF TOGETHER AND GIVE ME A FEW CLEAR ANSWERS.

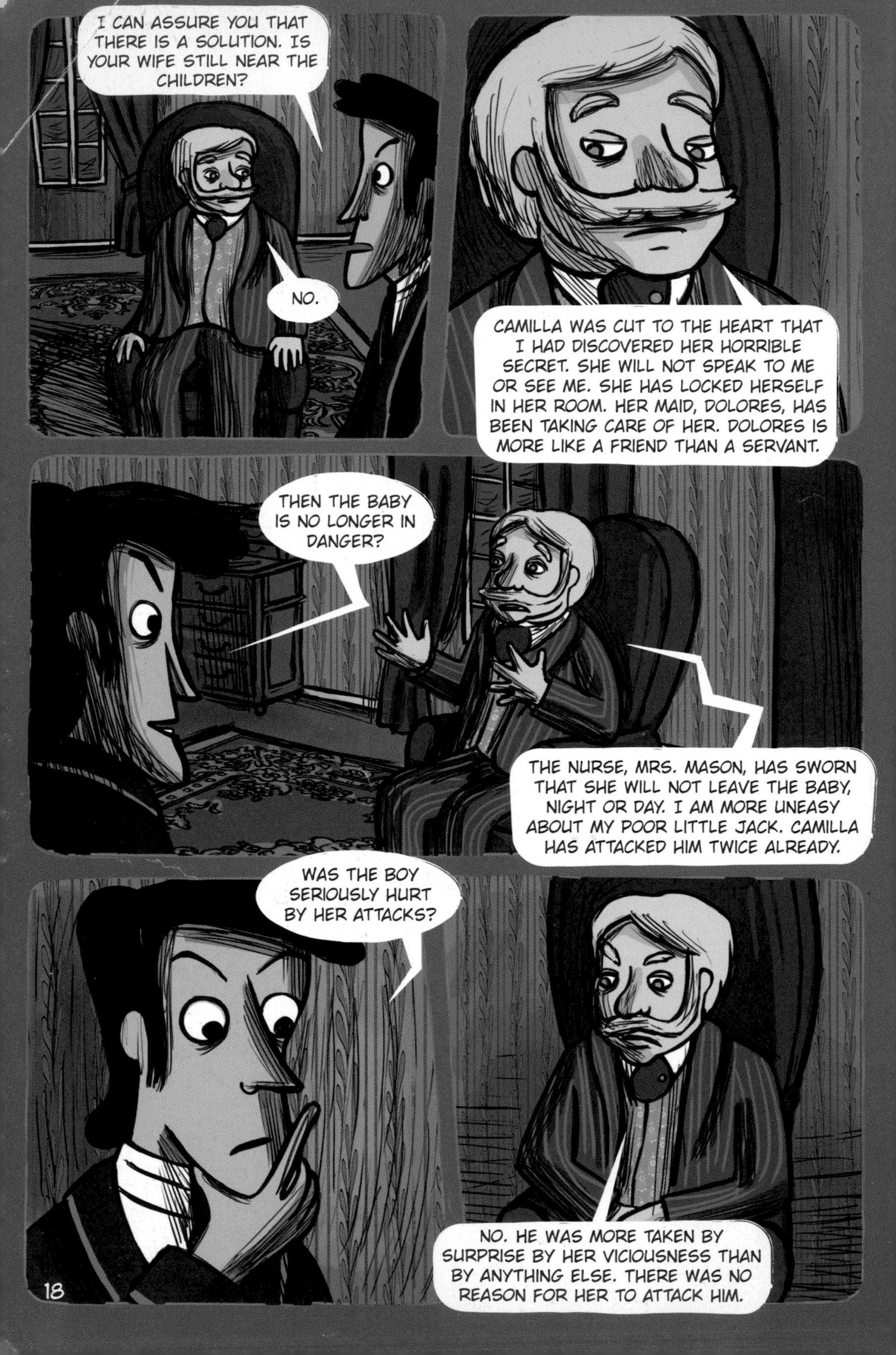
I CAN ASSURE YOU THAT THERE IS A SOLUTION. IS YOUR WIFE STILL NEAR THE CHILDREN?
NO.
CAMILLA WAS CUT TO THE HEART THAT I HAD DISCOVERED HER HORRIBLE SECRET. SHE WILL NOT SPEAK TO ME OR SEE ME. SHE HAS LOCKED HERSELF IN HER ROOM. HER MAID, DOLORES, HAS BEEN TAKING CARE OF HER. DOLORES IS MORE LIKE A FRIEND THAN A SERVANT.
THEN THE BABY IS NO LONGER IN DANGER?
THE NURSE, MRS. MASON, HAS SWORN THAT SHE WILL NOT LEAVE THE BABY, NIGHT OR DAY. I AM MORE UNEASY ABOUT MY POOR LITTLE JACK. CAMILLA HAS ATTACKED HIM TWICE ALREADY.
WAS THE BOY SERIOUSLY HURT BY HER ATTACKS?
NO. HE WAS MORE TAKEN BY SURPRISE BY HER VICIOUSNESS THAN BY ANYTHING ELSE. THERE WAS NO REASON FOR HER TO ATTACK HIM.

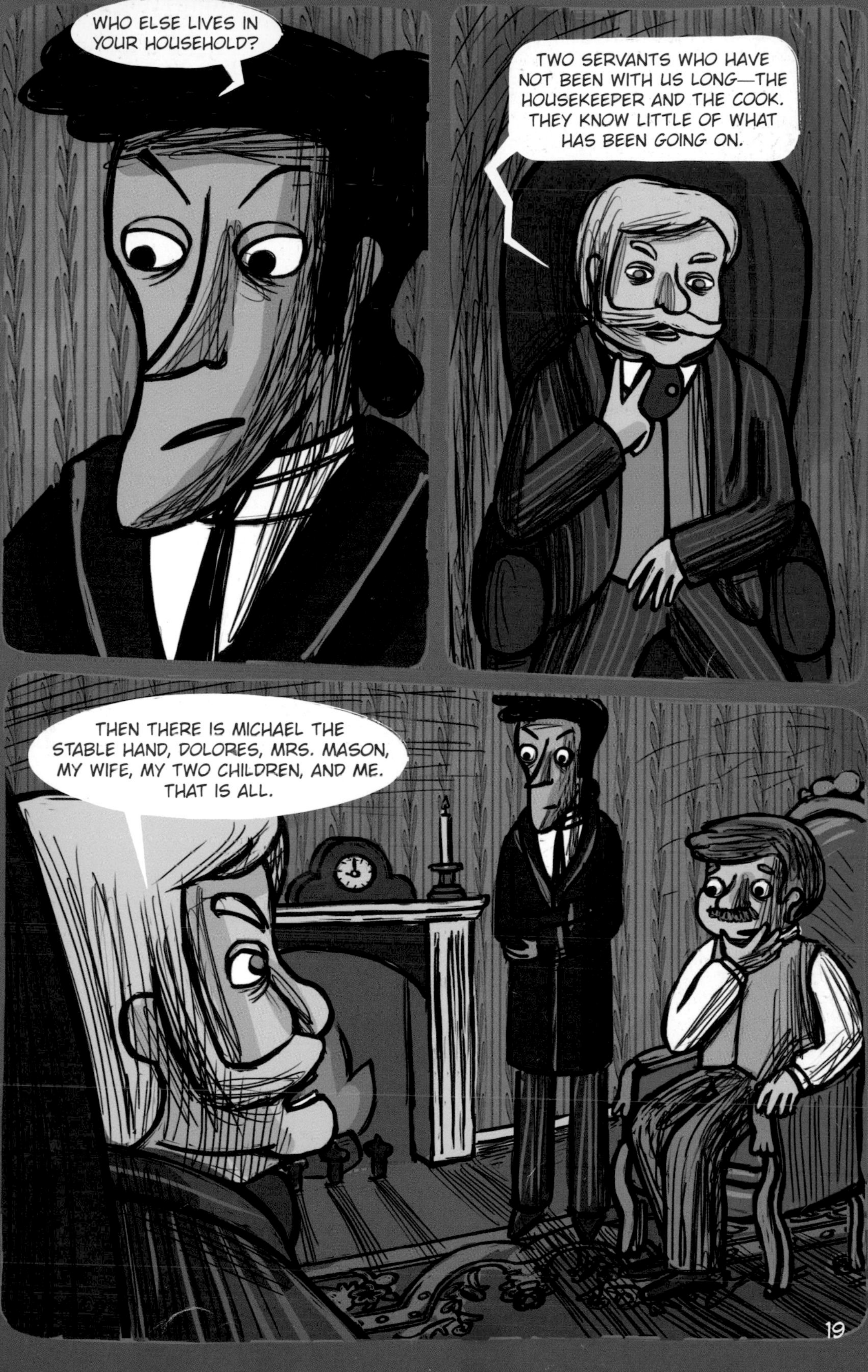
WHO ELSE LIVES IN YOUR HOUSEHOLD?
TWO SERVANTS WHO HAVE NOT BEEN WITH US LONG—THE HOUSEKEEPER AND THE COOK. THEY KNOW LITTLE OF WHAT HAS BEEN GOING ON.
THEN THERE IS MICHAEL THE STABLE HAND, DOLORES, MRS. MASON, MY WIFE, MY TWO CHILDREN, AND ME. THAT IS ALL.

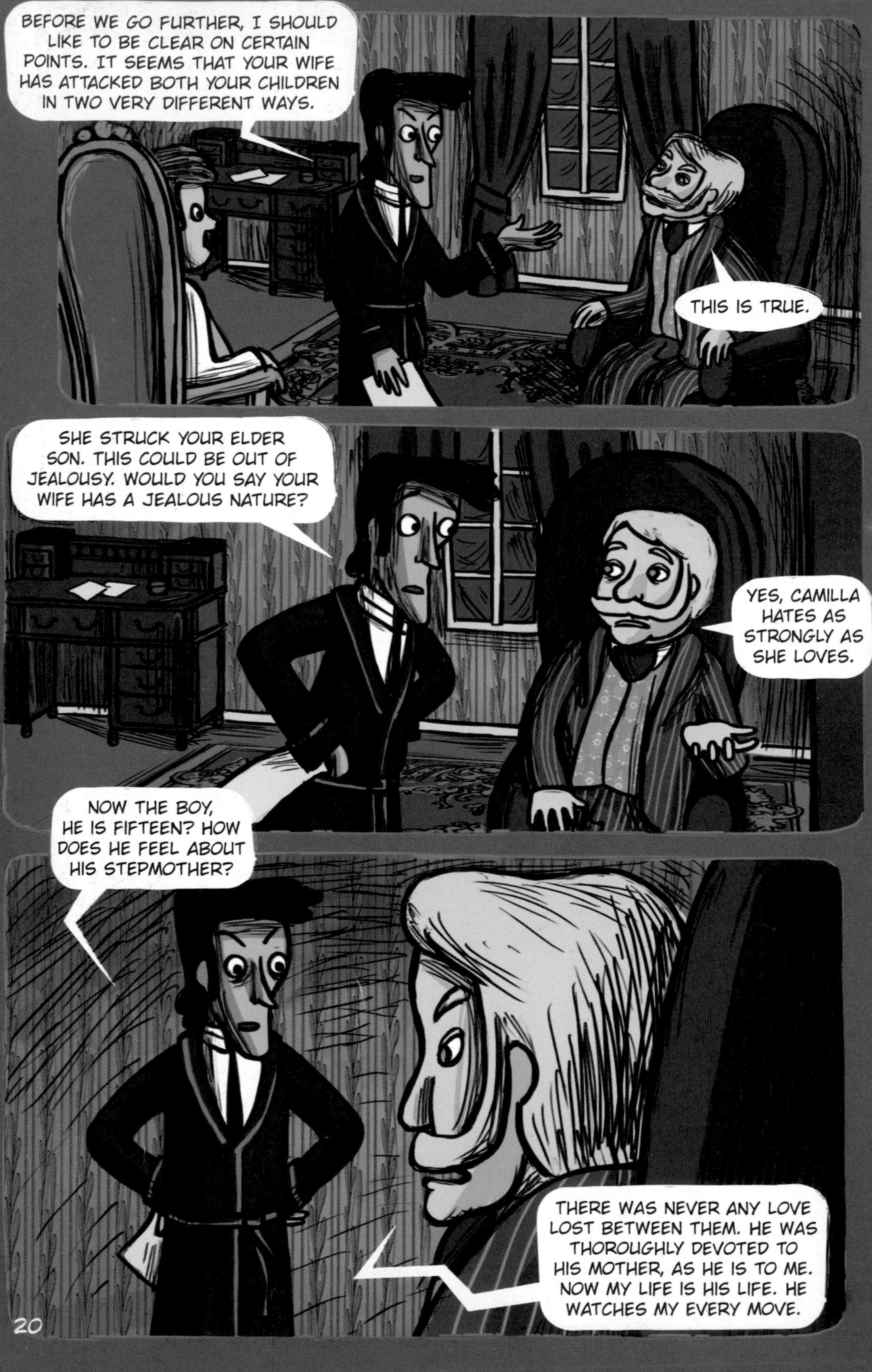
BEFORE WE GO FURTHER, I SHOULD LIKE TO BE CLEAR ON CERTAIN POINTS. IT SEEMS THAT YOUR WIFE HAS ATTACKED BOTH YOUR CHILDREN IN TWO VERY DIFFERENT WAYS.
THIS IS TRUE.
SHE STRUCK YOUR ELDER SON. THIS COULD BE OUT OF JEALOUSY. WOULD YOU SAY YOUR WIFE HAS A JEALOUS NATURE?
YES, CAMILLA HATES AS STRONGLY AS SHE LOVES.
NOW THE BOY, HE IS FIFTEEN? HOW DOES HE FEEL ABOUT HIS STEPMOTHER?
THERE WAS NEVER ANY LOVE LOST BETWEEN THEM. HE WAS THOROUGHLY DEVOTED TO HIS MOTHER, AS HE IS TO ME. NOW MY LIFE IS HIS LIFE. HE WATCHES MY EVERY MOVE.

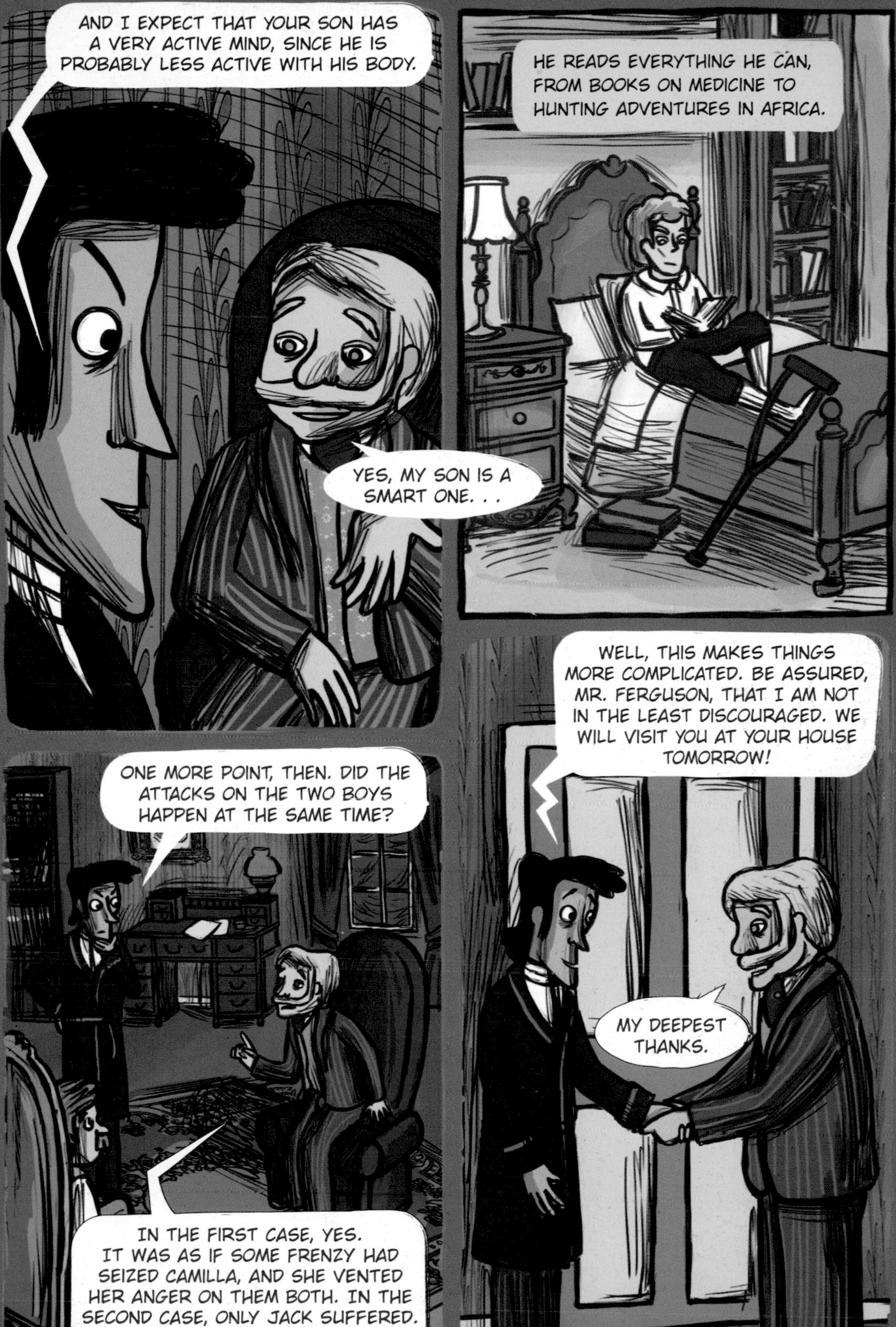
AND I EXPECT THAT YOUR SON HAS A VERY ACTIVE MIND, SINCE HE IS PROBABLY LESS ACTIVE WITH HIS BODY.
YES, MY SON IS A SMART ONE. . .
HE READS EVERYTHING HE CAN, FROM BOOKS ON MEDICINE TO HUNTING ADVENTURES IN AFRICA.
ONE MORE POINT, THEN. DID THE ATTACKS ON THE TWO BOYS HAPPEN AT THE SAME TIME?
IN THE FIRST CASE, YES. IT WAS AS IF SOME FRENZY HAD SEIZED CAMILLA, AND SHE VENTED HER ANGER ON THEM BOTH. IN THE SECOND CASE, ONLY JACK SUFFERED. AND IN THE THIRD, ONLY THE BABY.
WELL, THIS MAKES THINGS MORE COMPLICATED. BE ASSURED, MR. FERGUSON, THAT I AM NOT IN THE LEAST DISCOURAGED. WE WILL VISIT YOU AT YOUR HOUSE TOMORROW!
MY DEEPEST THANKS.

November 22, 4:00 p.m.

A dreary November fog had settled in. Having left our bags at the Lamberley Inn, we took a winding, muddy ride to Ferguson's ancient farmhouse locally known as the Cheeseman's. On the thick old wooden door was carved a picture of a man and a round of cheese. Ferguson led us into a large room with enormous oak beams and a huge, old-fashioned fireplace with a blazing fire. Yet the crumbling building gave off an odor of age and decay.

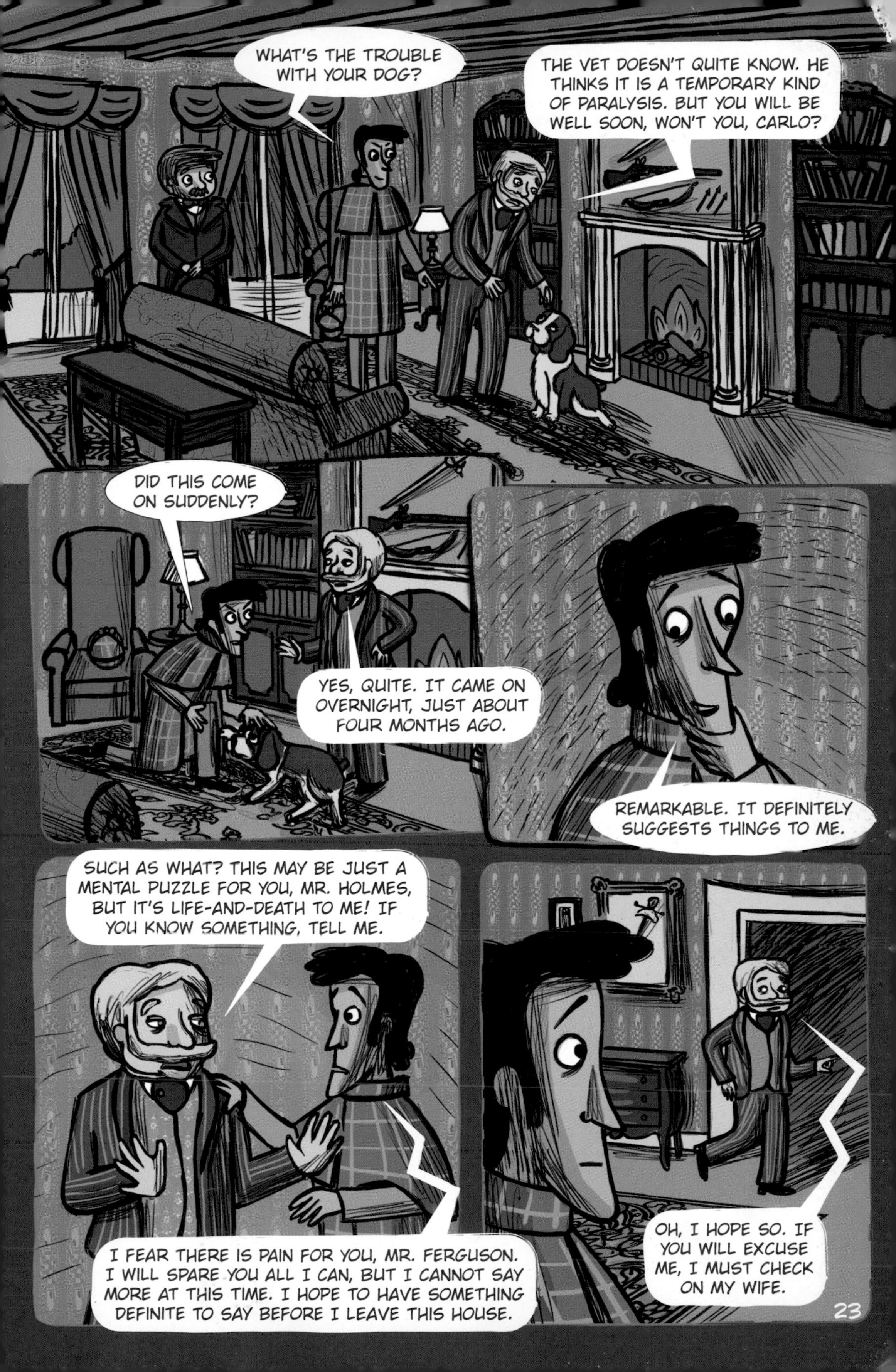
WHAT'S THE TROUBLE WITH YOUR DOG?
THE VET DOESN'T QUITE KNOW. HE THINKS IT IS A TEMPORARY KIND OF PARALYSIS. BUT YOU WILL BE WELL SOON, WON'T YOU, CARLO?
DID THIS COME ON SUDDENLY?
YES, QUITE. IT CAME ON OVERNIGHT, JUST ABOUT FOUR MONTHS AGO.
REMARKABLE. IT DEFINITELY SUGGESTS THINGS TO ME.
SUCH AS WHAT? THIS MAY BE JUST A MENTAL PUZZLE FOR YOU, MR. HOLMES, BUT IT'S LIFE-AND-DEATH TO ME! IF YOU KNOW SOMETHING, TELL ME.
I FEAR THERE IS PAIN FOR YOU, MR. FERGUSON. I WILL SPARE YOU ALL I CAN, BUT I CANNOT SAY MORE AT THIS TIME. I HOPE TO HAVE SOMETHING DEFINITE TO SAY BEFORE I LEAVE THIS HOUSE.
OH, I HOPE SO. IF YOU WILL EXCUSE ME, I MUST CHECK ON MY WIFE.

Our host left us, and Holmes began examining items in the room. I never tire of observing him at work. He walked around the room, peering closely at everything. He lifted and weighed objects in his hands, held them up to the light, and then gently replaced them. I could only imagine what he might be thinking.

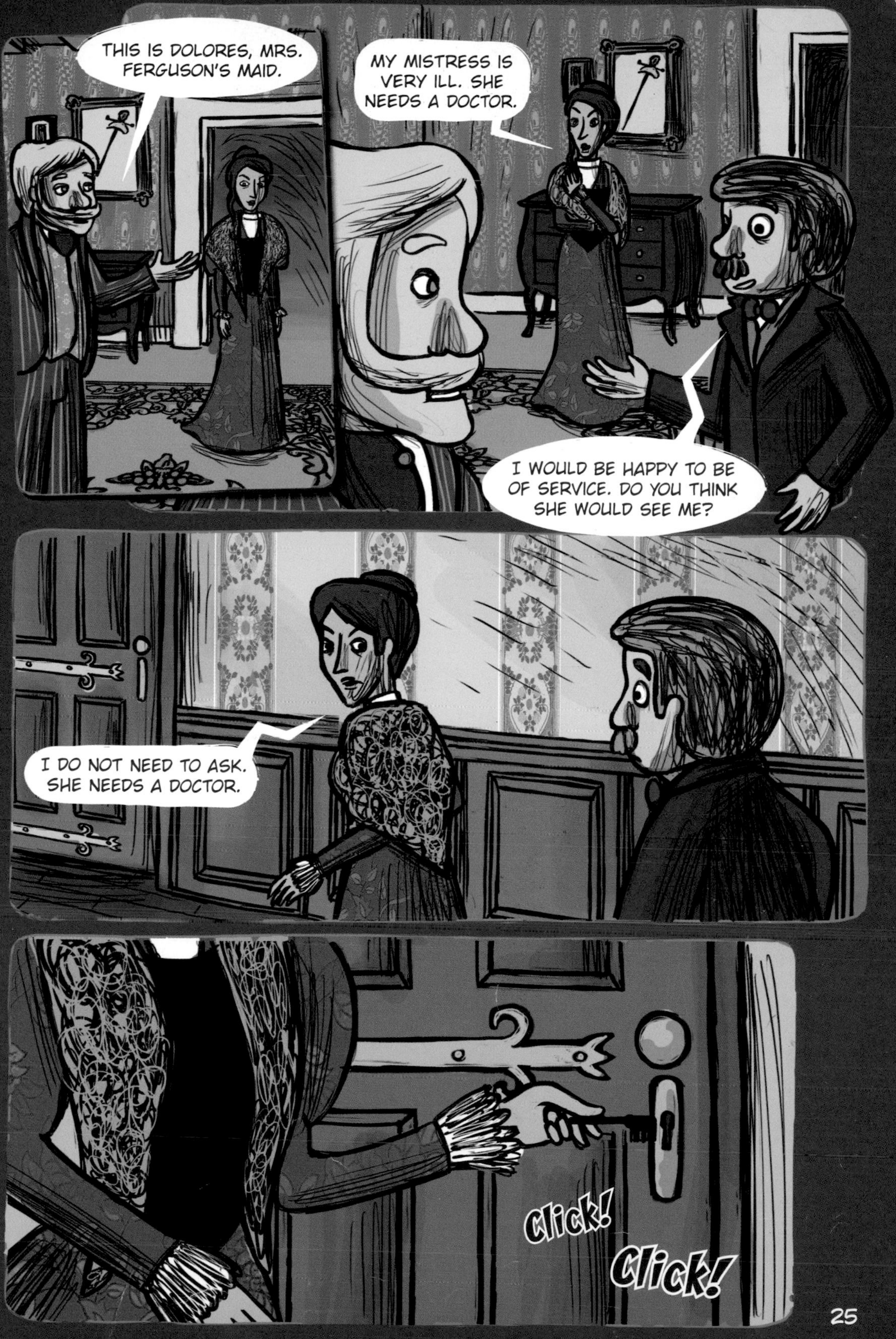
THIS IS DOLORES, MRS. FERGUSON'S MAID.
MY MISTRESS IS VERY ILL. SHE NEEDS A DOCTOR.
I WOULD BE HAPPY TO BE OF SERVICE. DO YOU THINK SHE WOULD SEE ME?
I DO NOT NEED TO ASK. SHE NEEDS A DOCTOR.
Click!
Click!

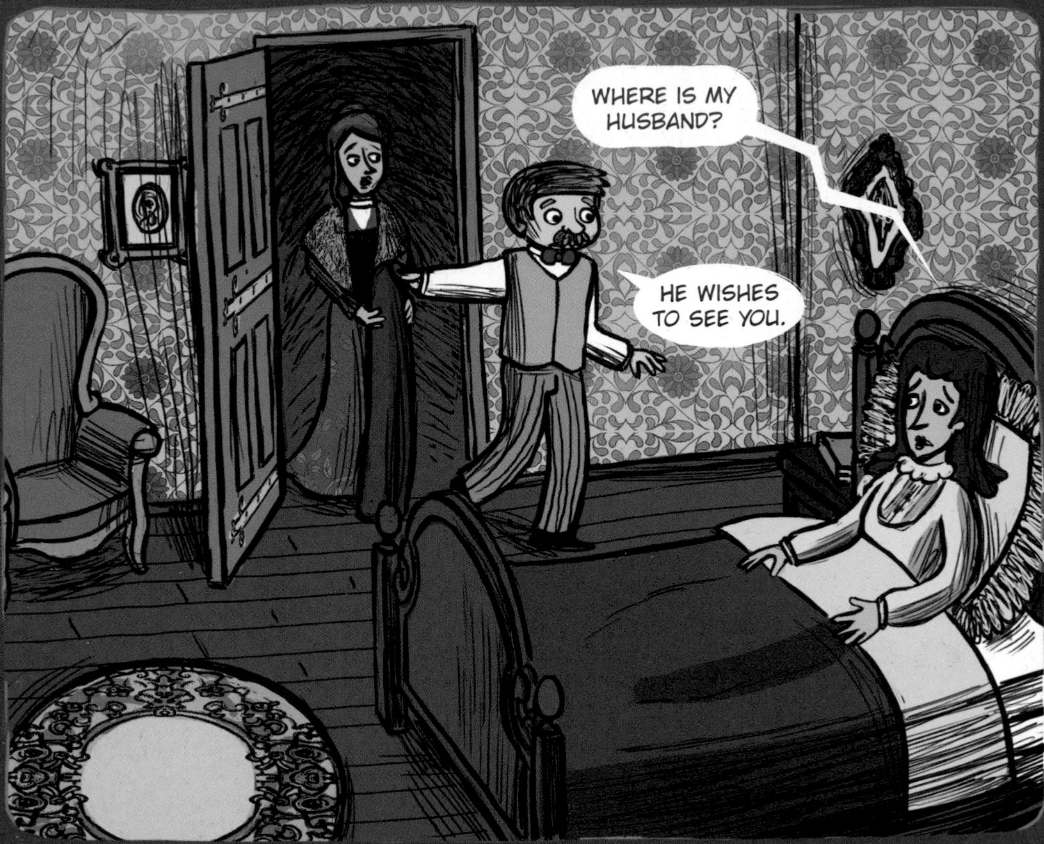
WHERE IS MY HUSBAND?
HE WISHES TO SEE YOU.

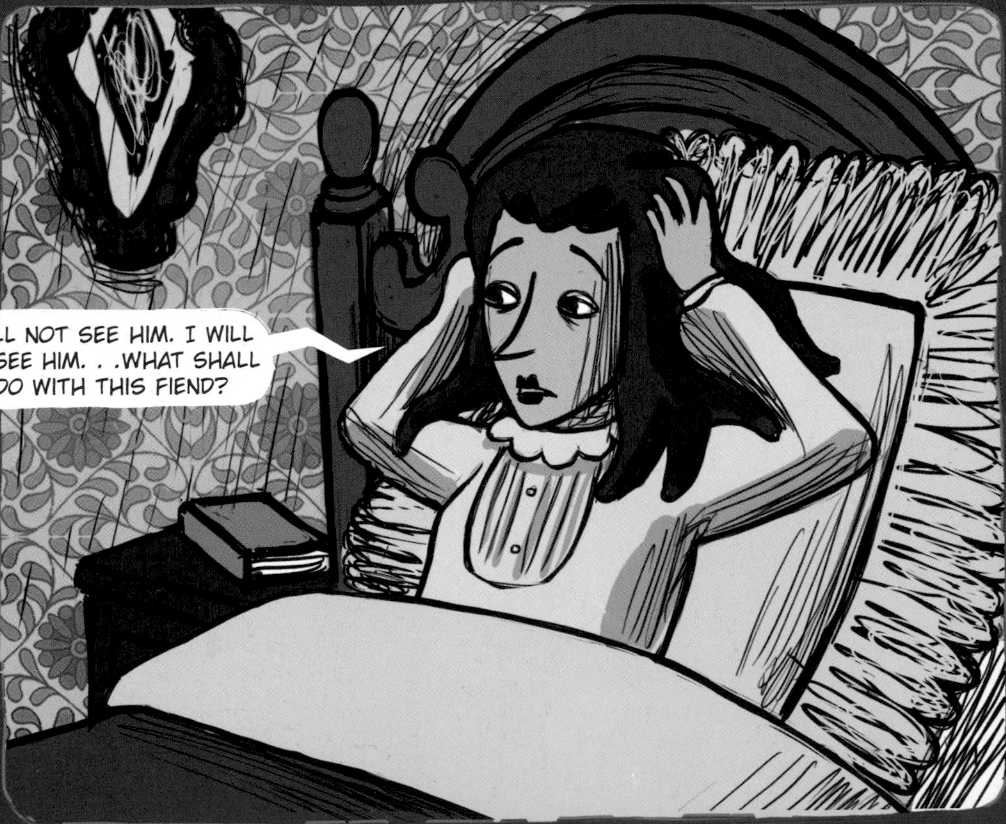
I WILL NOT SEE HIM. I WILL NOT SEE HIM. . .WHAT SHALL I DO WITH THIS FIEND?

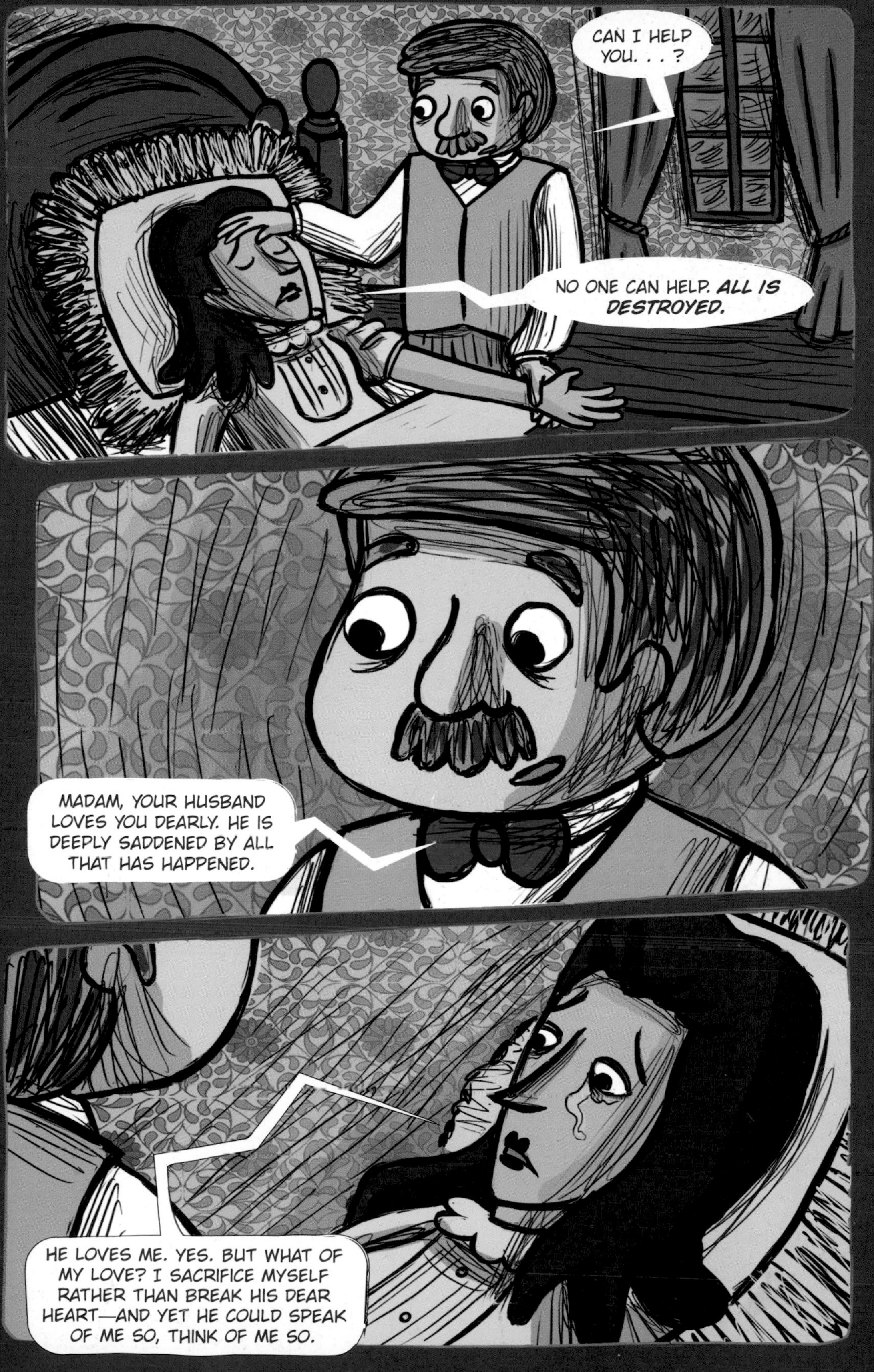
CAN I HELP YOU. . . ?
NO ONE CAN HELP. ALL IS DESTROYED.
MADAM, YOUR HUSBAND LOVES YOU DEARLY. HE IS DEEPLY SADDENED BY ALL THAT HAS HAPPENED.
HE LOVES ME. YES. BUT WHAT OF MY LOVE? I SACRIFICE MYSELF RATHER THAN BREAK HIS DEAR HEART—AND YET HE COULD SPEAK OF ME SO, THINK OF ME SO.

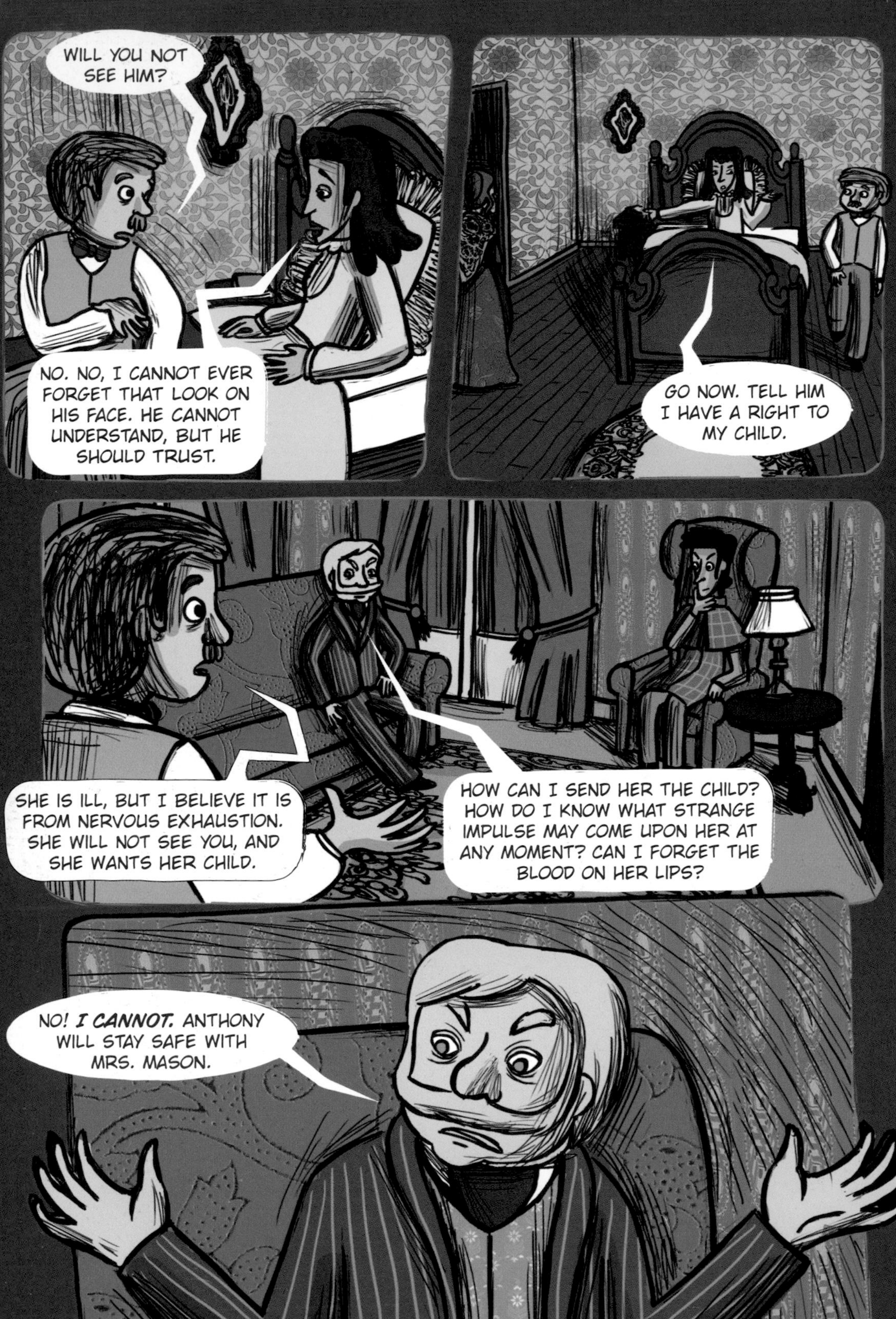

WILL YOU NOT SEE HIM?
NO. NO, I CANNOT EVER FORGET THAT LOOK ON HIS FACE. HE CANNOT UNDERSTAND, BUT HE SHOULD TRUST.
GO NOW. TELL HIM I HAVE A RIGHT TO MY CHILD.
SHE IS ILL, BUT I BELIEVE IT IS FROM NERVOUS EXHAUSTION. SHE WILL NOT SEE YOU, AND SHE WANTS HER CHILD.
HOW CAN I SEND HER THE CHILD? HOW DO I KNOW WHAT STRANGE IMPULSE MAY COME UPON HER AT ANY MOMENT? CAN I FORGET THE BLOOD ON HER LIPS?
NO! I CANNOT. ANTHONY WILL STAY SAFE WITH MRS. MASON.

Holmes said not a word. Shortly, Ferguson collected himself enough to look up and observe a servant standing in the doorway with the tea service. He bade her to come and serve us. We sat down and began to sip our tea, and Ferguson seemed to calm ever so slightly.

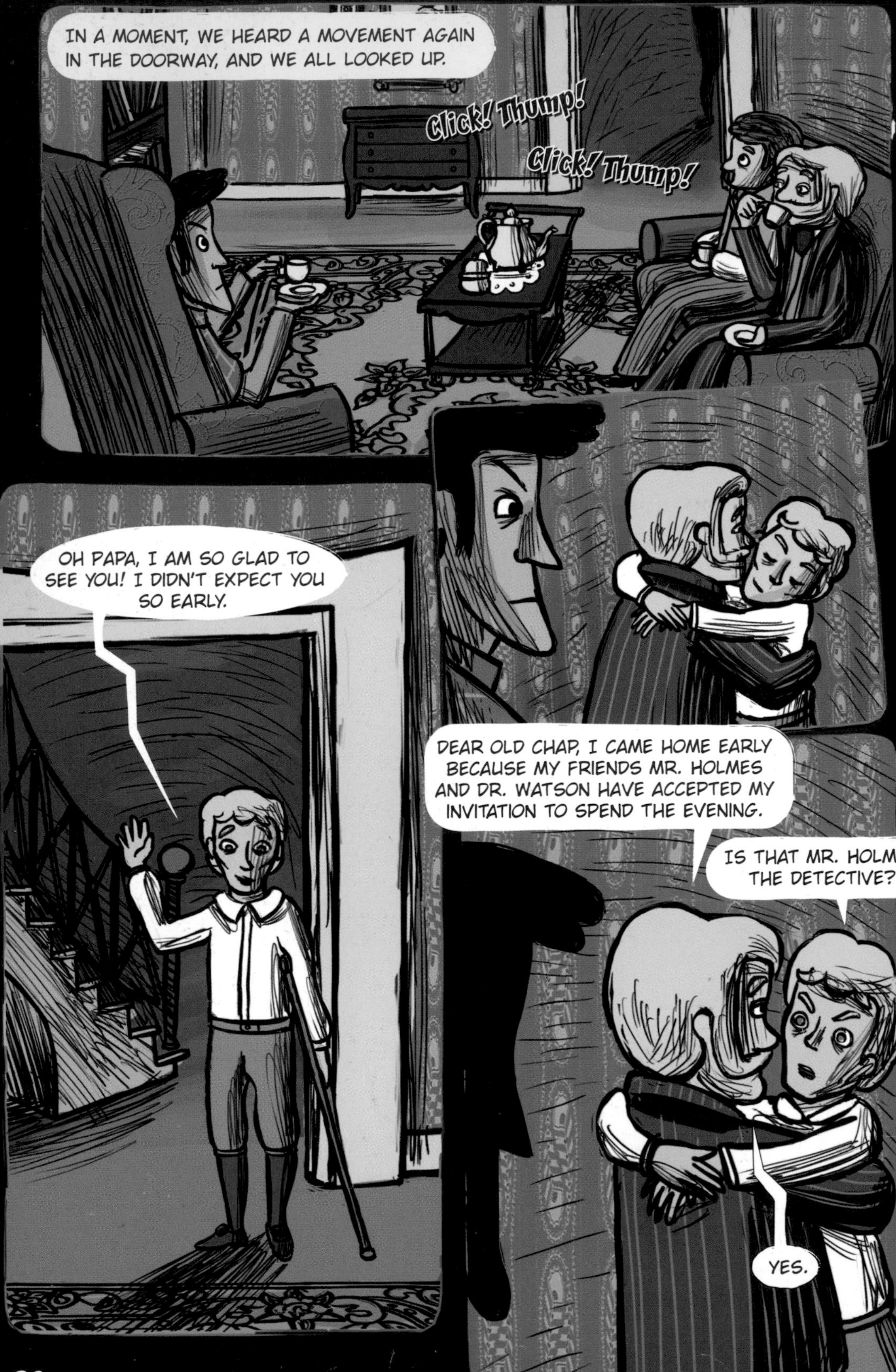
IN A MOMENT, WE HEARD A MOVEMENT AGAIN IN THE DOORWAY, AND WE ALL LOOKED UP.
Click! Thump!
Click! Thump!
OH PAPA, I AM SO GLAD TO SEE YOU! I DIDN'T EXPECT YOU SO EARLY.
DEAR OLD CHAP, I CAME HOME EARLY BECAUSE MY FRIENDS MR. HOLMES AND DR. WATSON HAVE ACCEPTED MY INVITATION TO SPEND THE EVENING.
IS THAT MR. HOLMES THE DETECTIVE?
YES.

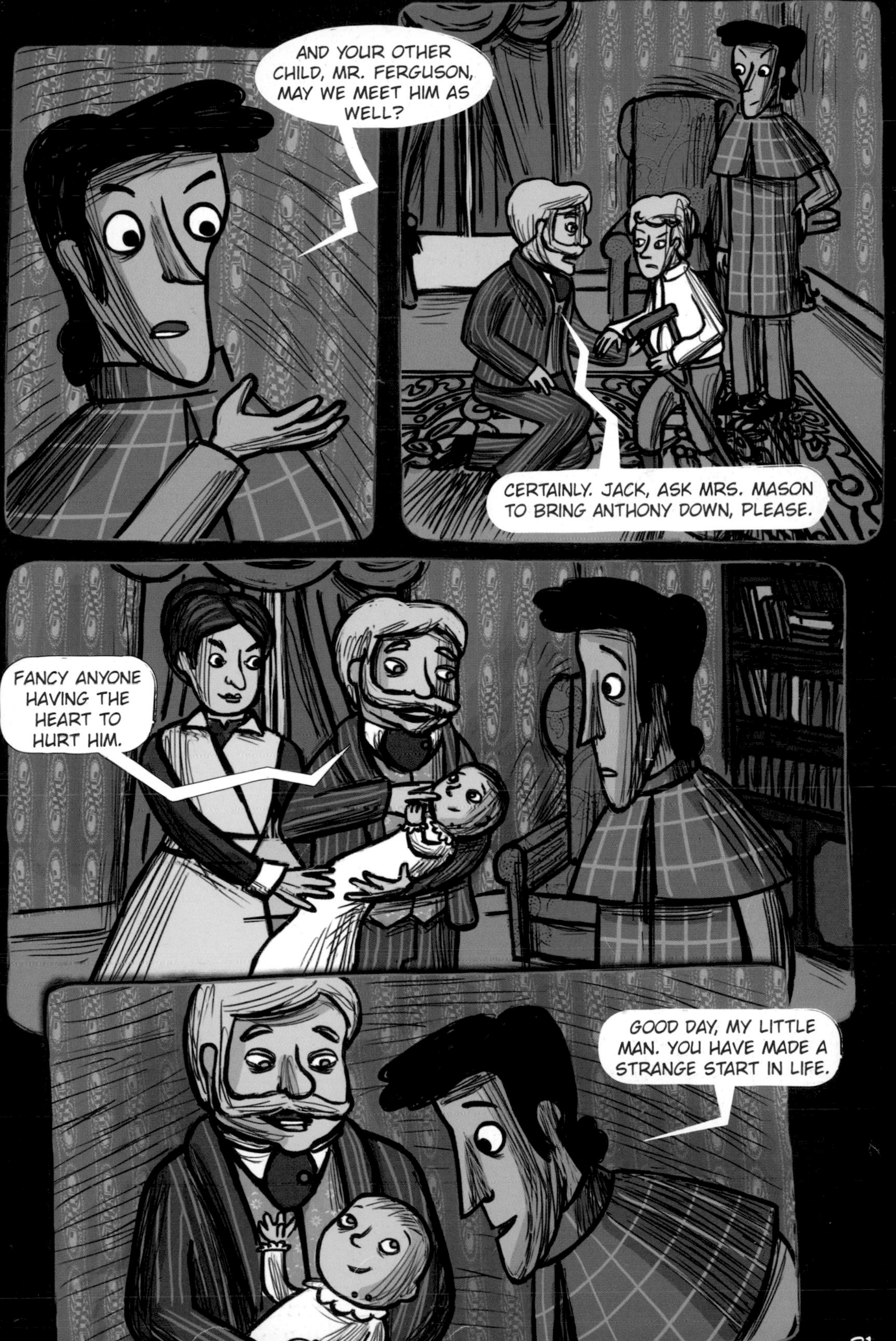
AND YOUR OTHER CHILD, MR. FERGUSON, MAY WE MEET HIM AS WELL?
CERTAINLY. JACK, ASK MRS. MASON TO BRING ANTHONY DOWN, PLEASE.
FANCY ANYONE HAVING THE HEART TO HURT HIM.
GOOD DAY, MY LITTLE MAN. YOU HAVE MADE A STRANGE START IN LIFE.

As we stood with the child, I chanced to glance at Holmes. His intent eyes and hawk nose were set as if they had been carved in ivory. His eyes had taken in father and child. They had then moved with eager curiosity on to something at the far edge of the room.

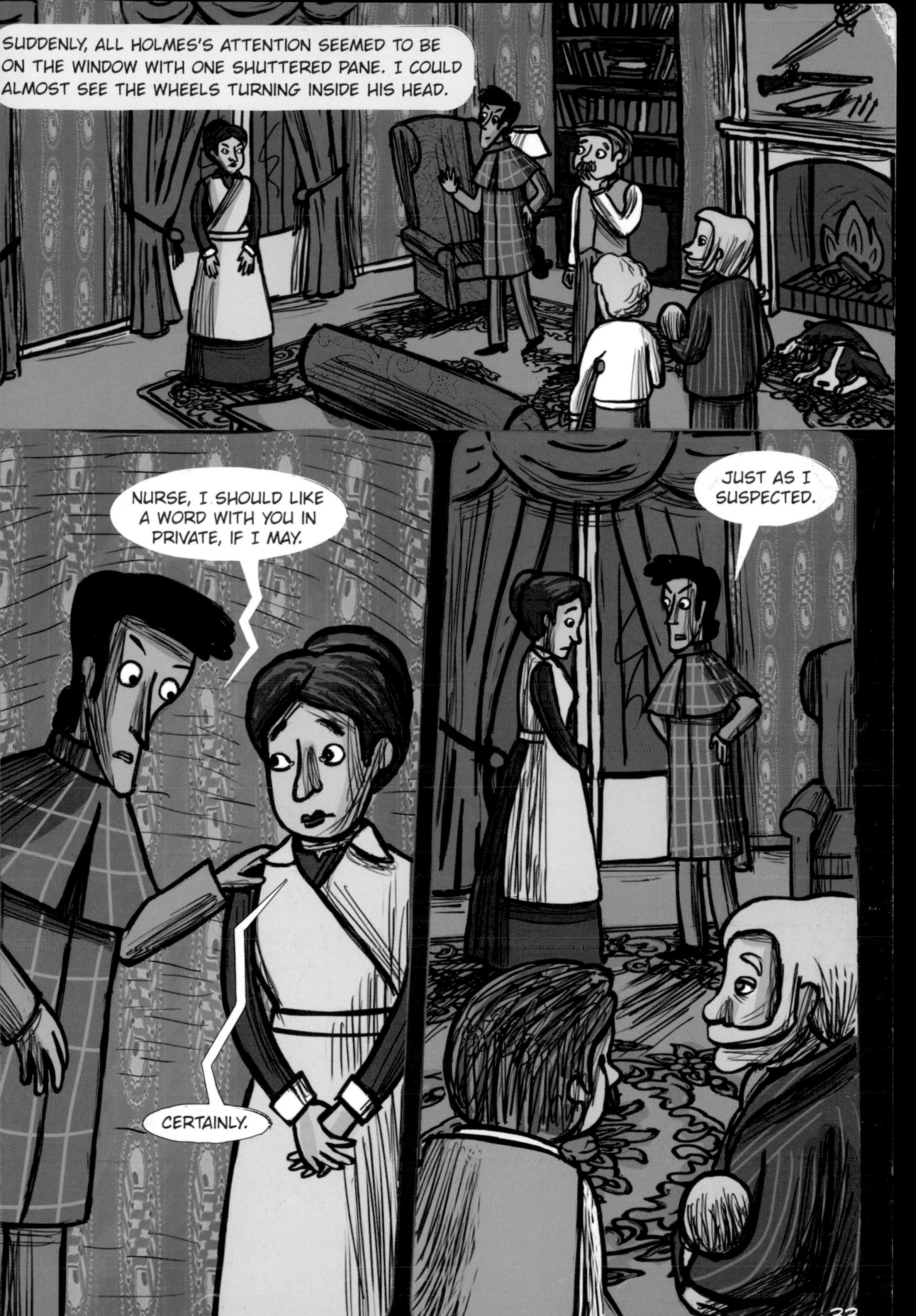
SUDDENLY, ALL HOLMES'S ATTENTION SEEMED TO BE ON THE WINDOW WITH ONE SHUTTERED PANE. I COULD ALMOST SEE THE WHEELS TURNING INSIDE HIS HEAD.
NURSE, I SHOULD LIKE A WORD WITH YOU IN PRIVATE, IF I MAY.
CERTAINLY.
JUST AS I SUSPECTED.

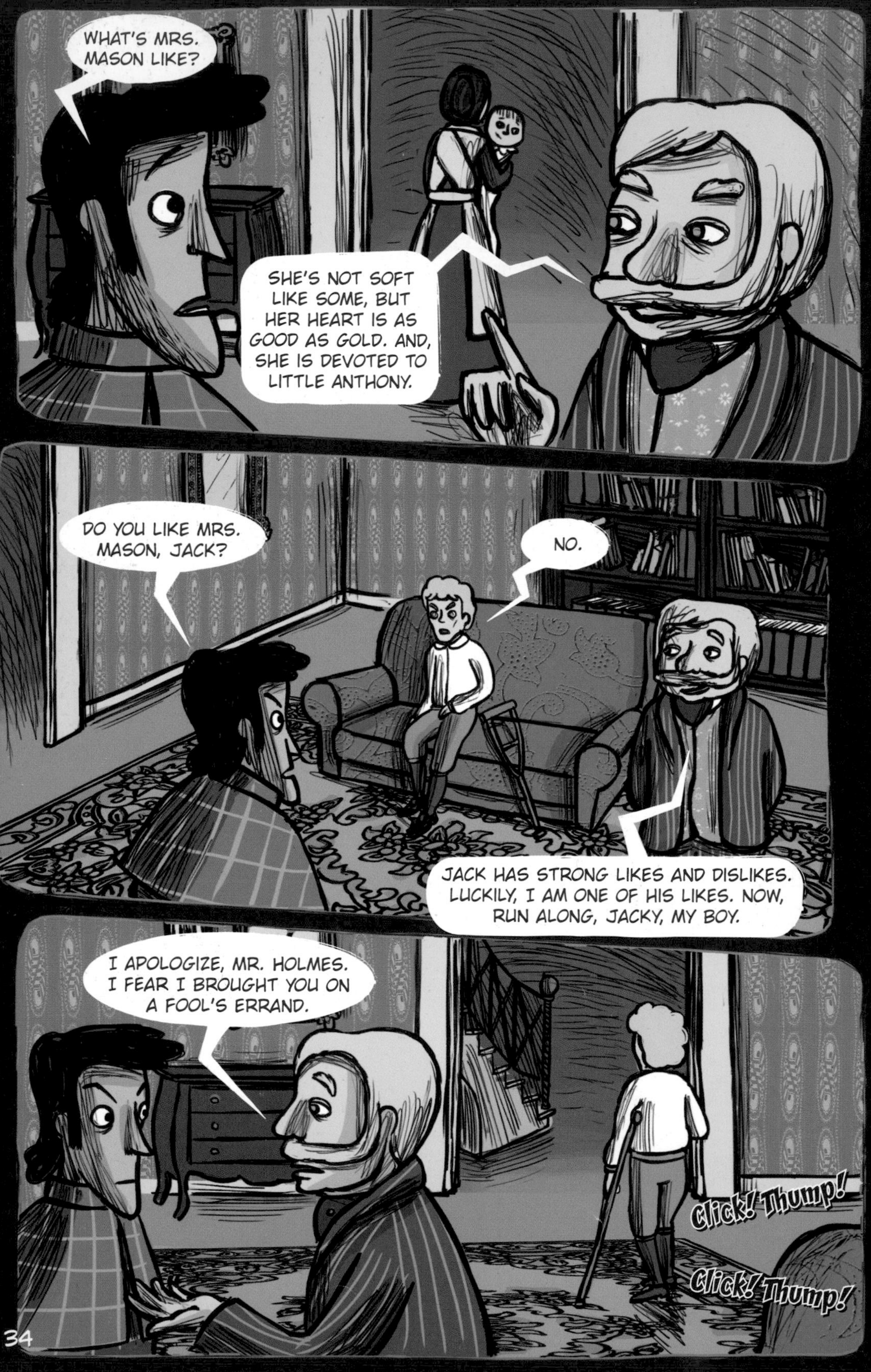
WHAT'S MRS. MASON LIKE?
SHE'S NOT SOFT LIKE SOME, BUT HER HEART IS AS GOOD AS GOLD. AND, SHE IS DEVOTED TO LITTLE ANTHONY.
DO YOU LIKE MRS. MASON, JACK?
NO.
JACK HAS STRONG LIKES AND DISLIKES. LUCKILY, I AM ONE OF HIS LIKES. NOW, RUN ALONG, JACKY, MY BOY.
I APOLOGIZE, MR. HOLMES. I FEAR I BROUGHT YOU ON A FOOL'S ERRAND.
Click! Thump!
Click! Thump!

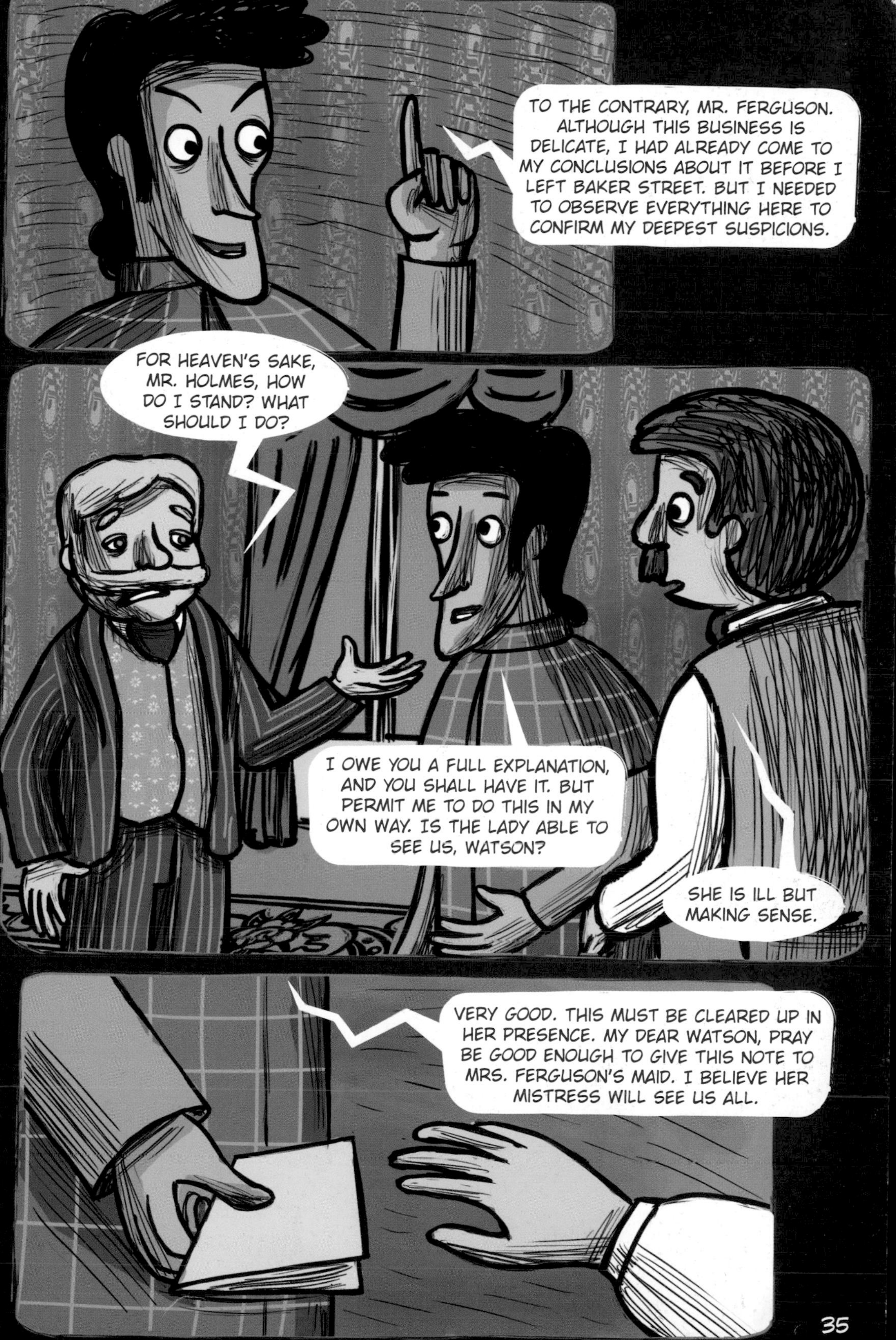
TO THE CONTRARY, MR. FERGUSON. ALTHOUGH THIS BUSINESS IS DELICATE, I HAD ALREADY COME TO MY CONCLUSIONS ABOUT IT BEFORE I LEFT BAKER STREET. BUT I NEEDED TO OBSERVE EVERYTHING HERE TO CONFIRM MY DEEPEST SUSPICIONS.
FOR HEAVEN'S SAKE, MR. HOLMES, HOW DO I STAND? WHAT SHOULD I DO?
I OWE YOU A FULL EXPLANATION, AND YOU SHALL HAVE IT. BUT PERMIT ME TO DO THIS IN MY OWN WAY. IS THE LADY ABLE TO SEE US, WATSON?
SHE IS ILL BUT MAKING SENSE.
VERY GOOD. THIS MUST BE CLEARED UP IN HER PRESENCE. MY DEAR WATSON, PRAY BE GOOD ENOUGH TO GIVE THIS NOTE TO MRS. FERGUSON'S MAID. I BELIEVE HER MISTRESS WILL SEE US ALL.

I had not viewed Holmes penning the note since our arrival, and I could not imagine what it might say. Nevertheless, I returned to the heavy oak door and passed the note to Dolores. A moment or two later, I heard a cry from within the room. It held a mixture of joy and surprise.

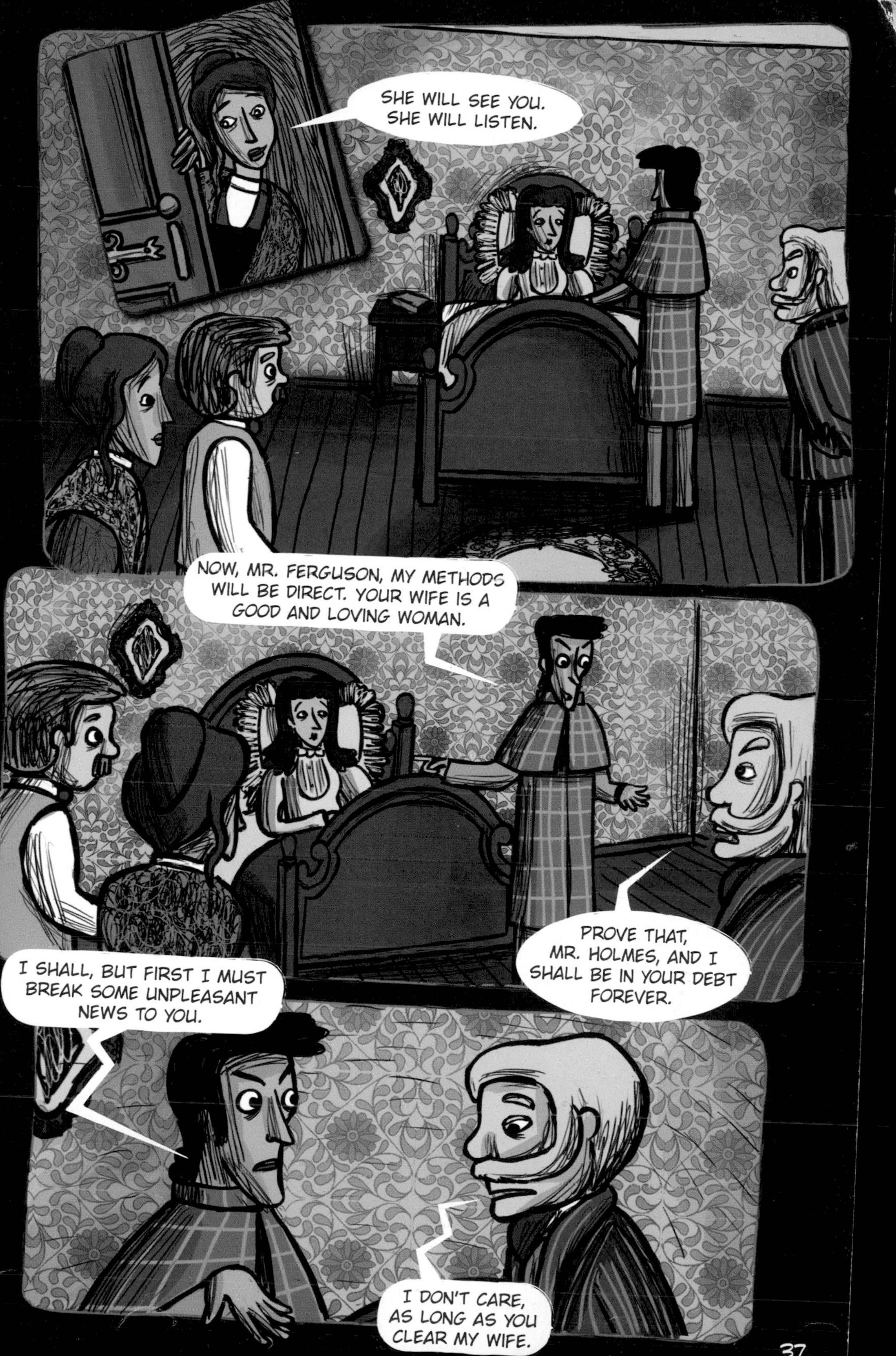
SHE WILL SEE YOU. SHE WILL LISTEN.
NOW, MR. FERGUSON, MY METHODS WILL BE DIRECT. YOUR WIFE IS A GOOD AND LOVING WOMAN.
PROVE THAT, MR. HOLMES, AND I SHALL BE IN YOUR DEBT FOREVER.
I SHALL, BUT FIRST I MUST BREAK SOME UNPLEASANT NEWS TO YOU.
I DON'T CARE, AS LONG AS YOU CLEAR MY WIFE.

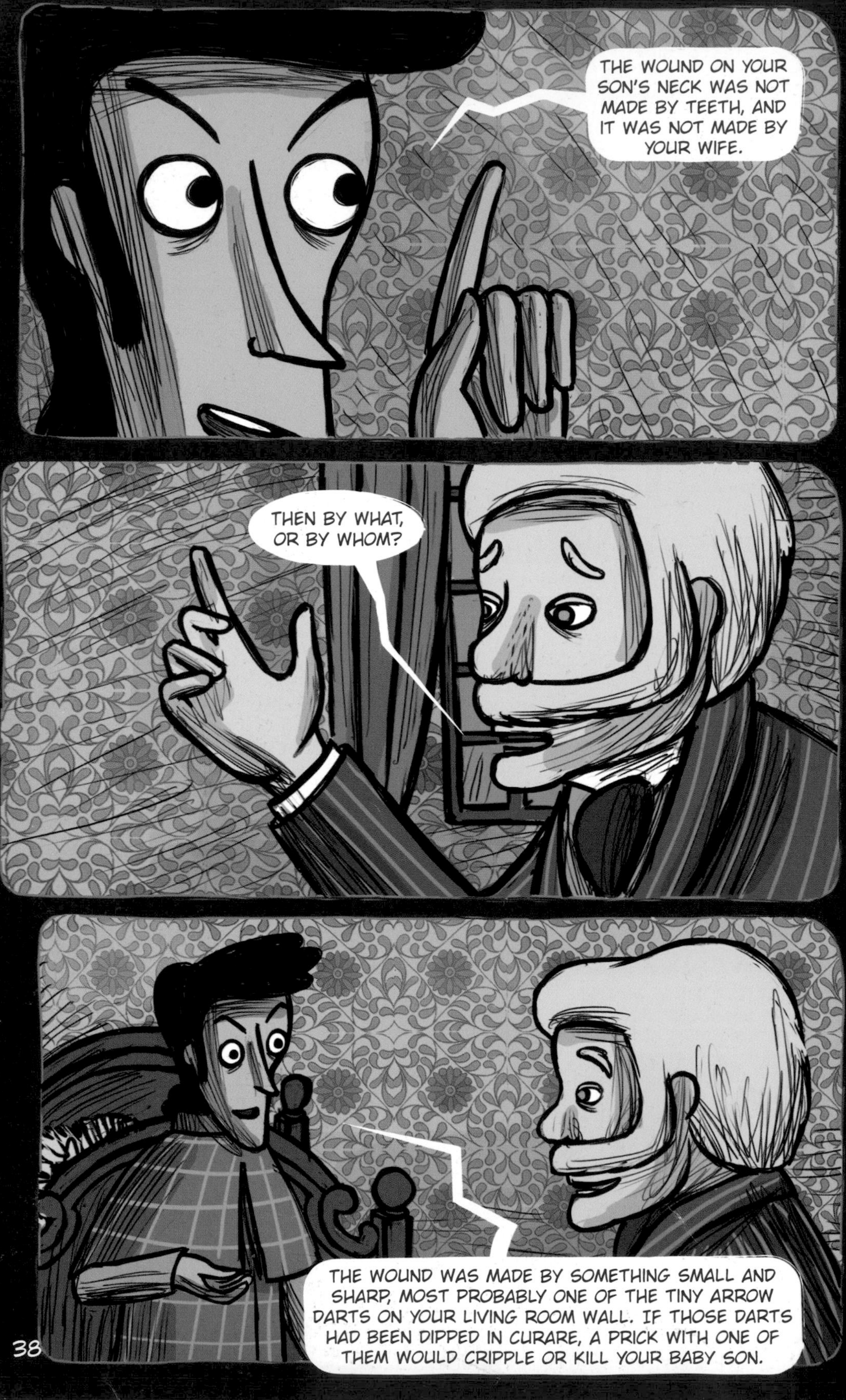
THE WOUND ON YOUR SON'S NECK WAS NOT MADE BY TEETH, AND IT WAS NOT MADE BY YOUR WIFE.
THEN BY WHAT, OR BY WHOM?
THE WOUND WAS MADE BY SOMETHING SMALL AND SHARP, MOST PROBABLY ONE OF THE TINY ARROW DARTS ON YOUR LIVING ROOM WALL. IF THOSE DARTS HAD BEEN DIPPED IN CURARE, A PRICK WITH ONE OF THEM WOULD CRIPPLE OR KILL YOUR BABY SON.

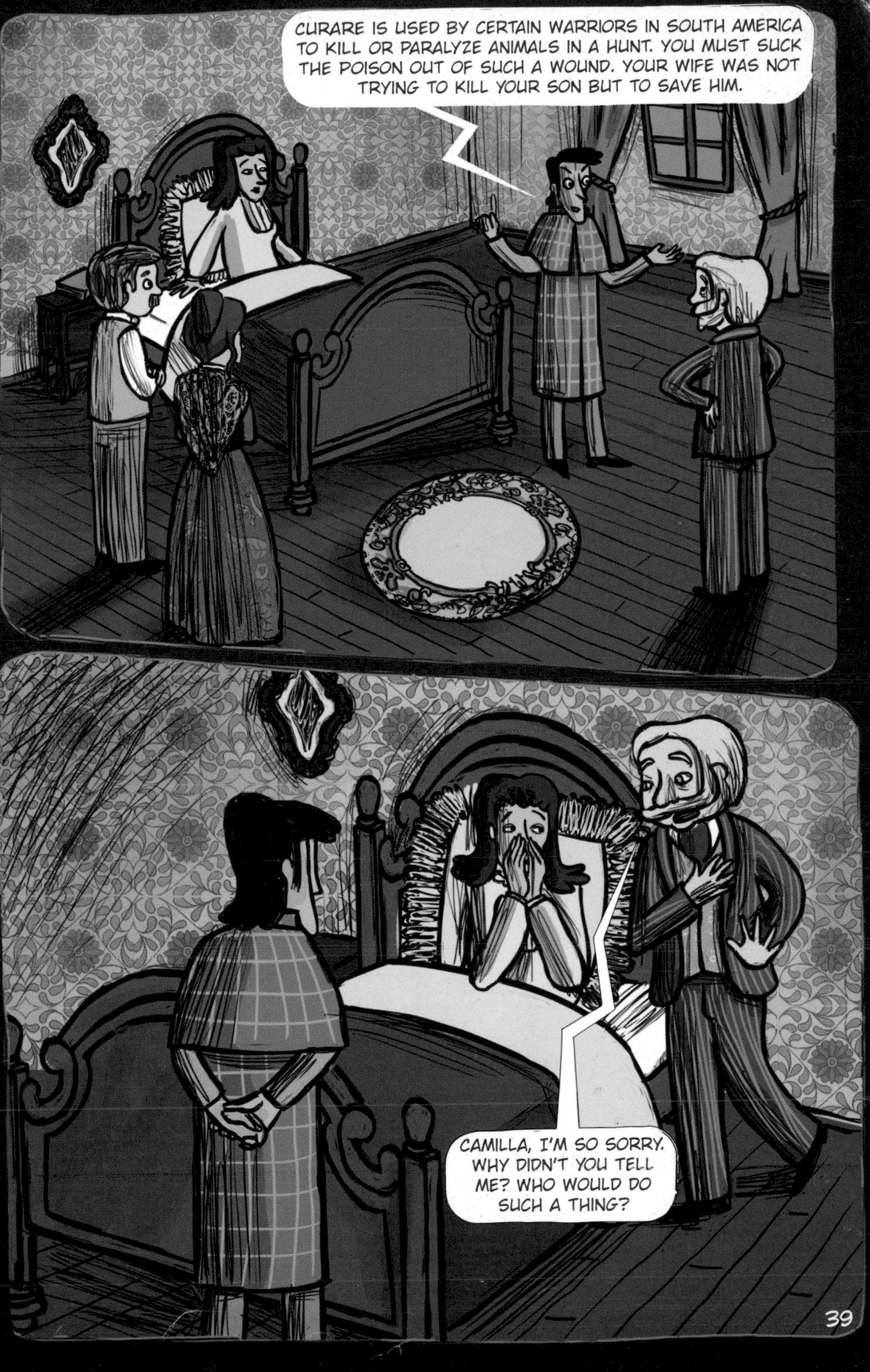
CURARE IS USED BY CERTAIN WARRIORS IN SOUTH AMERICA TO KILL OR PARALYZE ANIMALS IN A HUNT. YOU MUST SUCK THE POISON OUT OF SUCH A WOUND. YOUR WIFE WAS NOT TRYING TO KILL YOUR SON BUT TO SAVE HIM.
CAMILLA, I'M SO SORRY. WHY DIDN'T YOU TELL ME? WHO WOULD DO SUCH A THING?

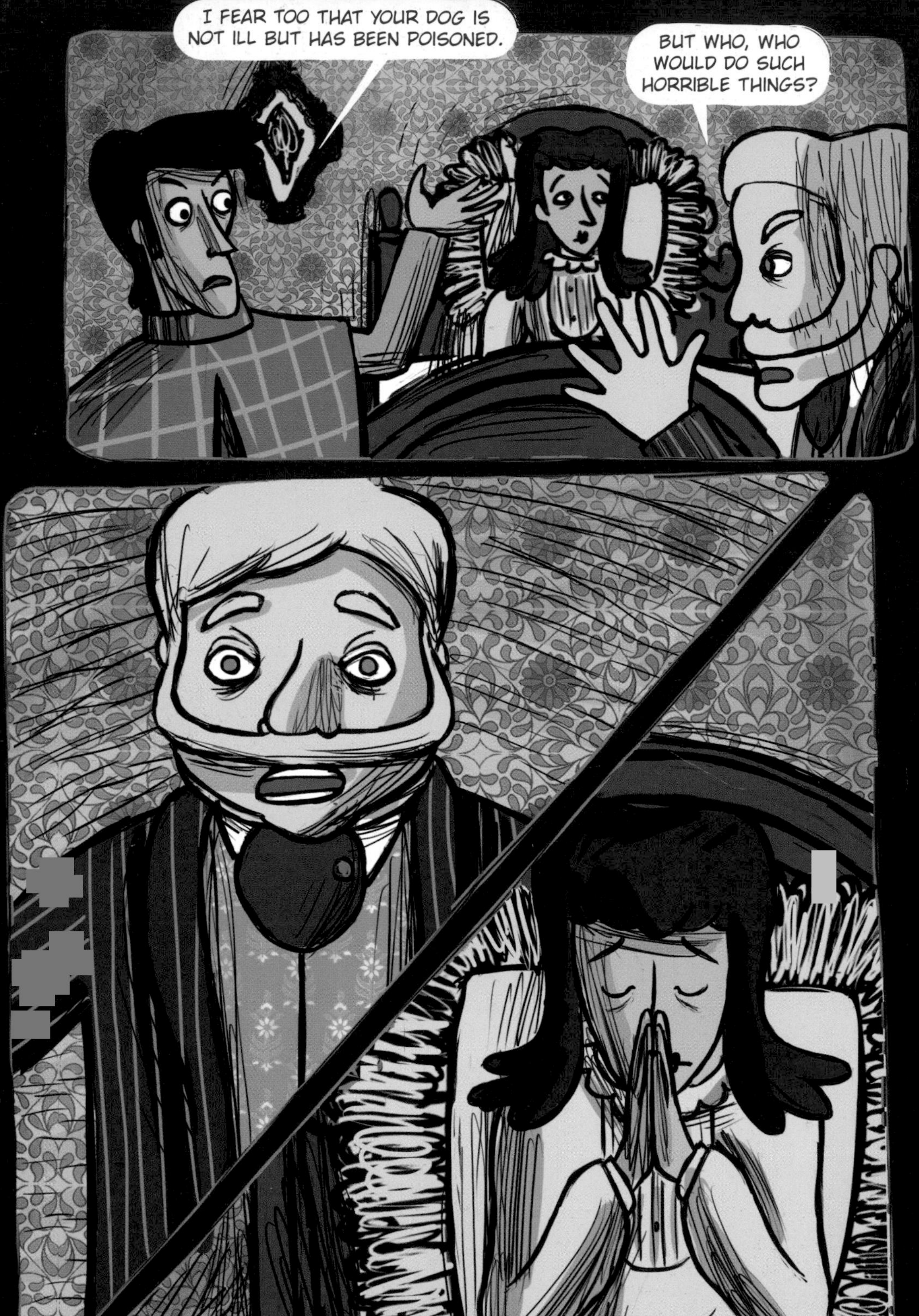
I FEAR TOO THAT YOUR DOG IS NOT ILL BUT HAS BEEN POISONED.
BUT WHO, WHO WOULD DO SUCH HORRIBLE THINGS?

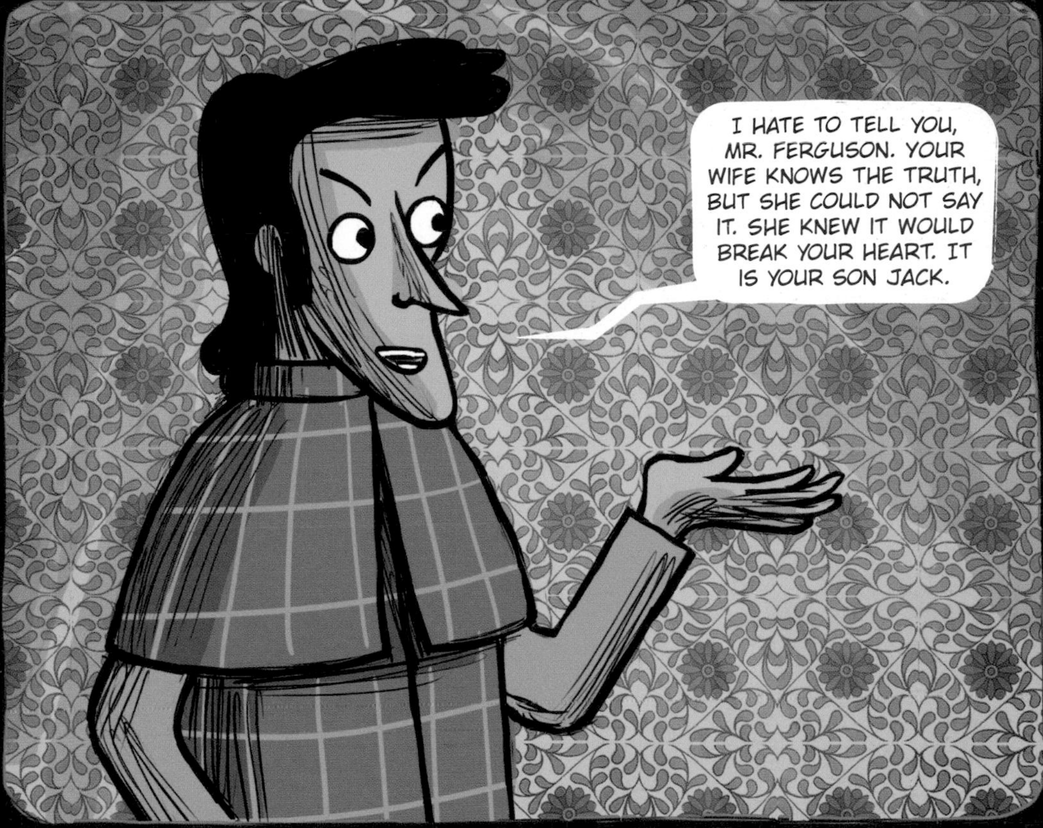
I HATE TO TELL YOU, MR. FERGUSON. YOUR WIFE KNOWS THE TRUTH, BUT SHE COULD NOT SAY IT. SHE KNEW IT WOULD BREAK YOUR HEART. IT IS YOUR SON JACK.

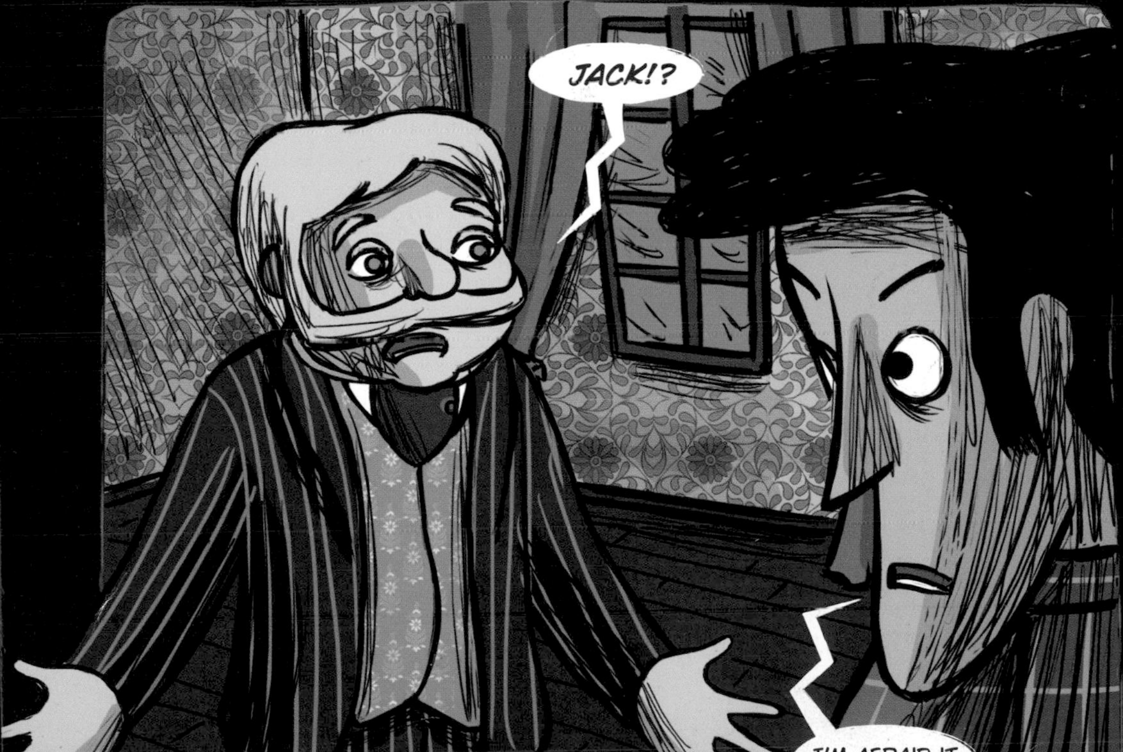
JACK!?
I'M AFRAID IT IS SO. . .

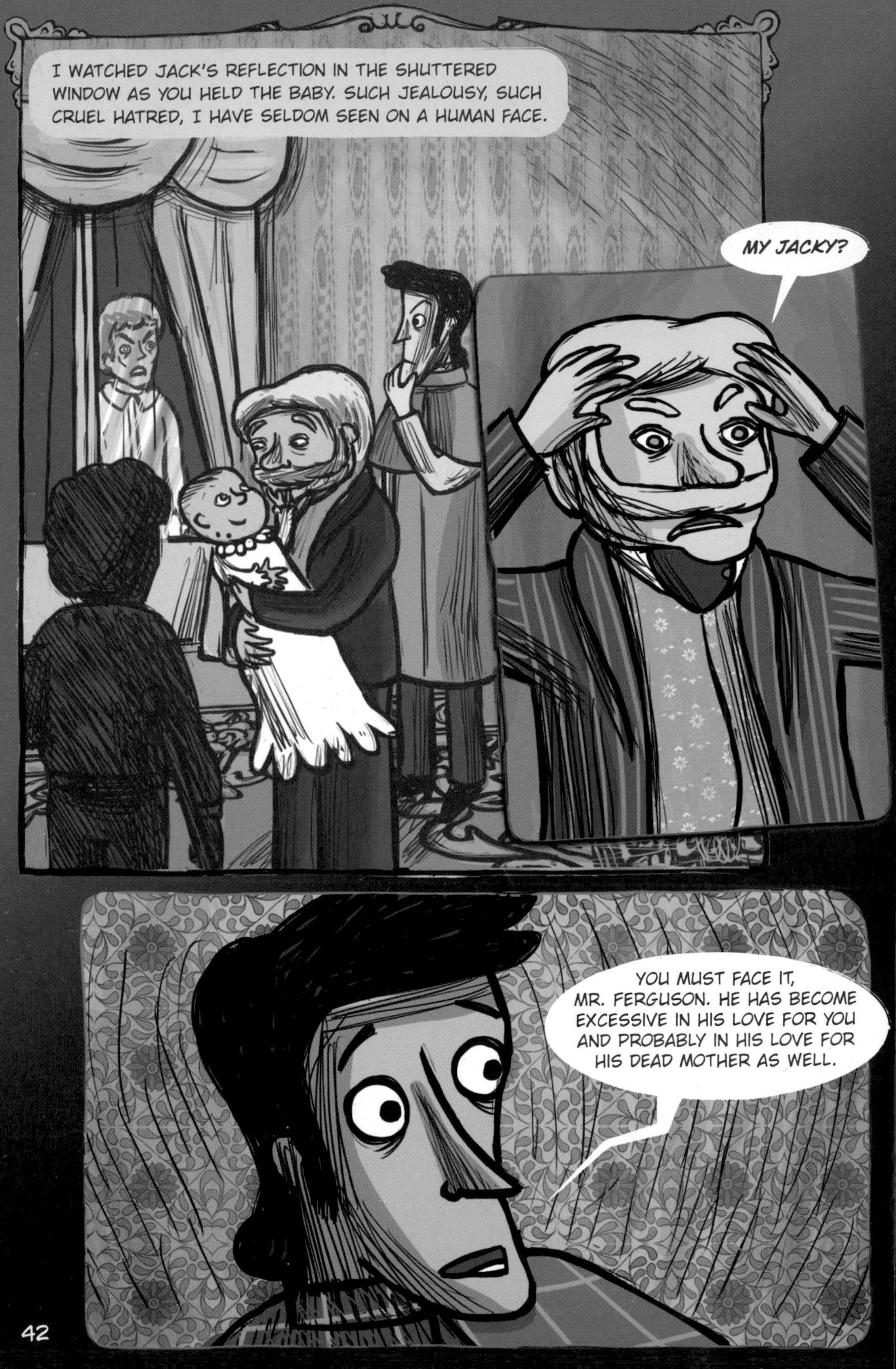
I WATCHED JACK'S REFLECTION IN THE SHUTTERED WINDOW AS YOU HELD THE BABY. SUCH JEALOUSY, SUCH CRUEL HATRED, I HAVE SELDOM SEEN ON A HUMAN FACE.
MY JACKY?
YOU MUST FACE IT, MR. FERGUSON. HE HAS BECOME EXCESSIVE IN HIS LOVE FOR YOU AND PROBABLY IN HIS LOVE FOR HIS DEAD MOTHER AS WELL.

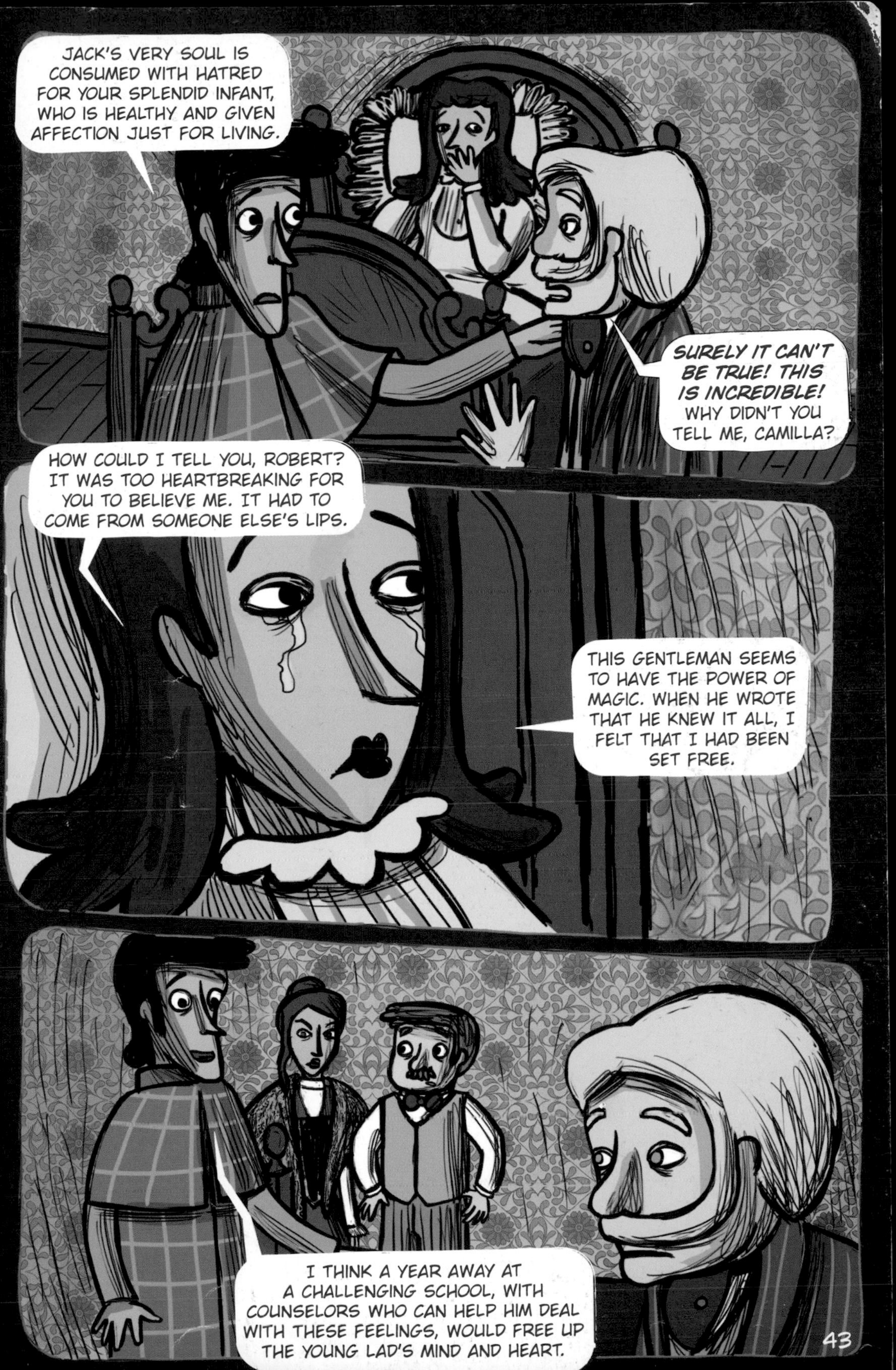
JACK'S VERY SOUL IS CONSUMED WITH HATRED FOR YOUR SPLENDID INFANT, WHO IS HEALTHY AND GIVEN AFFECTION JUST FOR LIVING.
SURELY IT CAN'T BE TRUE! THIS IS INCREDIBLE! WHY DIDN'T YOU TELL ME, CAMILLA?
HOW COULD I TELL YOU, ROBERT? IT WAS TOO HEARTBREAKING FOR YOU TO BELIEVE ME. IT HAD TO COME FROM SOMEONE ELSE'S LIPS.
THIS GENTLEMAN SEEMS TO HAVE THE POWER OF MAGIC. WHEN HE WROTE THAT HE KNEW IT ALL, I FELT THAT I HAD BEEN SET FREE.
I THINK A YEAR AWAY AT A CHALLENGING SCHOOL, WITH COUNSELORS WHO CAN HELP HIM DEAL WITH THESE FEELINGS, WOULD FREE UP THE YOUNG LAD'S MIND AND HEART.

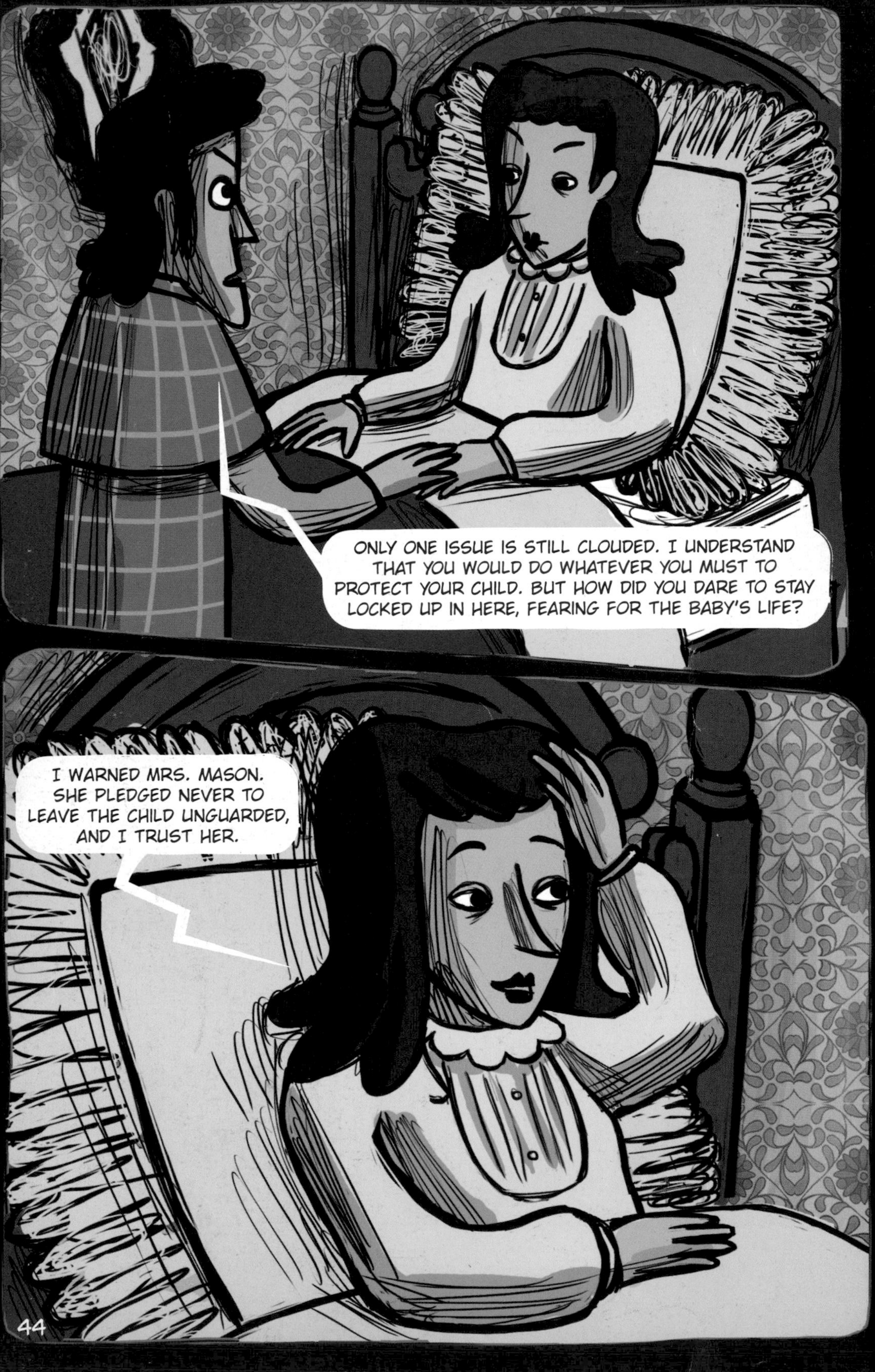
ONLY ONE ISSUE IS STILL CLOUDED. I UNDERSTAND THAT YOU WOULD DO WHATEVER YOU MUST TO PROTECT YOUR CHILD. BUT HOW DID YOU DARE TO STAY LOCKED UP IN HERE, FEARING FOR THE BABY'S LIFE?
I WARNED MRS. MASON. SHE PLEDGED NEVER TO LEAVE THE CHILD UNGUARDED, AND I TRUST HER.

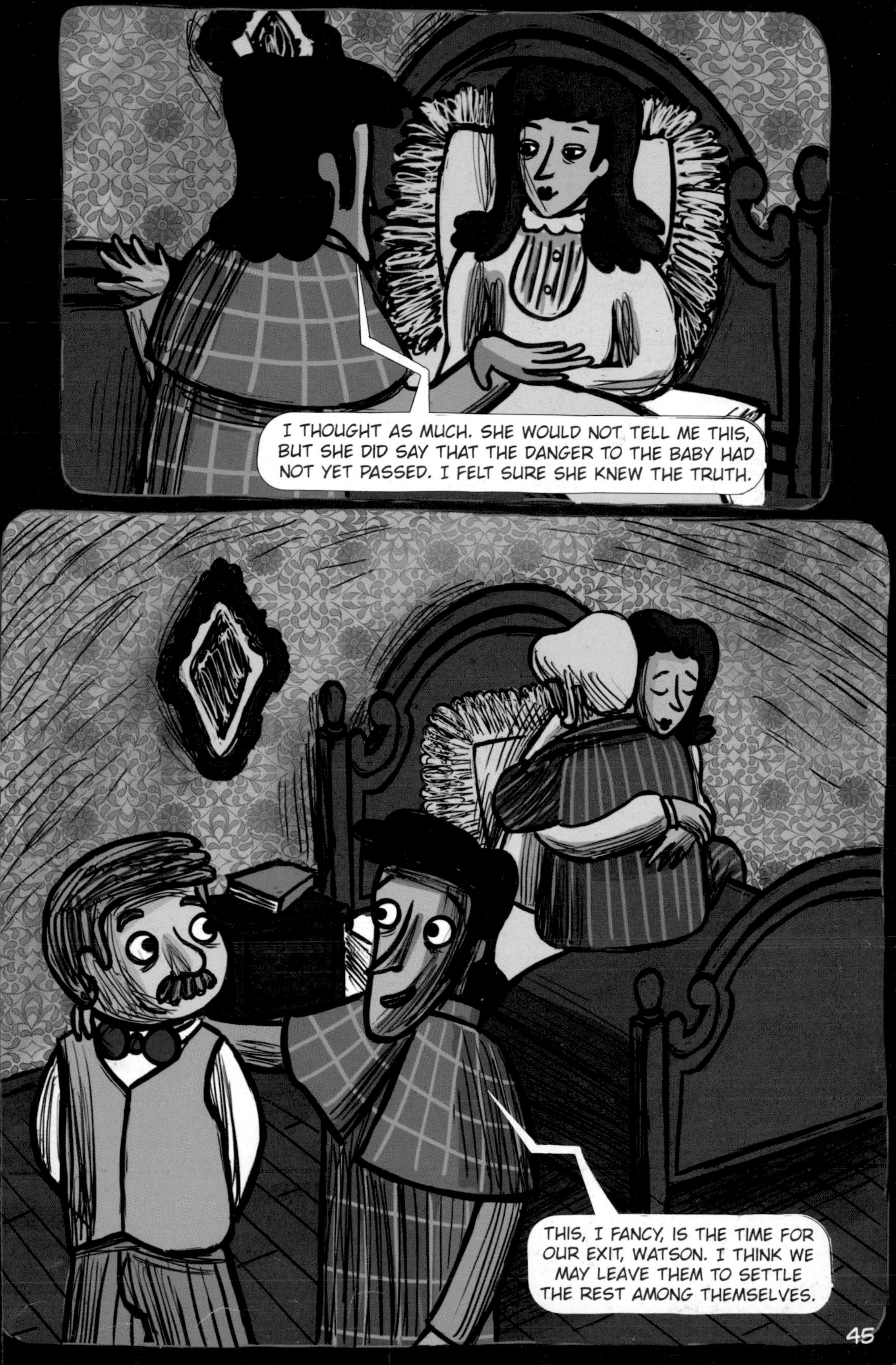
I THOUGHT AS MUCH. SHE WOULD NOT TELL ME THIS, BUT SHE DID SAY THAT THE DANGER TO THE BABY HAD NOT YET PASSED. I FELT SURE SHE KNEW THE TRUTH.
THIS, I FANCY, IS THE TIME FOR OUR EXIT, WATSON. I THINK WE MAY LEAVE THEM TO SETTLE THE REST AMONG THEMSELVES.

From the Desk of
John H. Watson, M.D.

The Adventure of the Sussex Vampire: How Did Holmes Solve It?

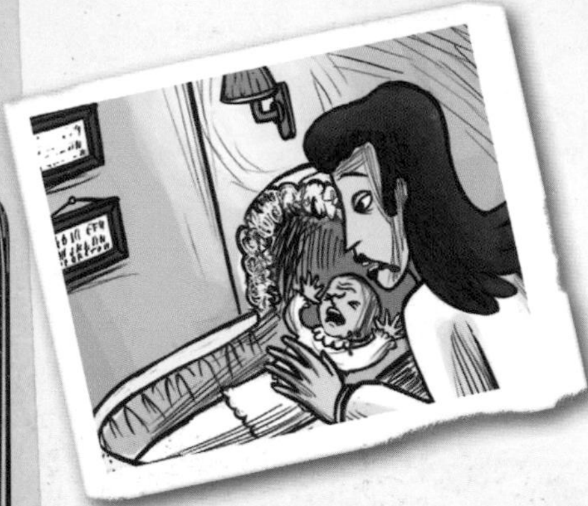

How did Holmes know Mrs. Ferguson wasn't a vampire?

The idea of a vampire seemed absurd to Sherlock Holmes. So he needed another theory. He figured that Mrs. Ferguson could have been trying to draw a poison out of the wound on her son's neck, rather than blood.

Why did Holmes suspect Jack was the poisoner?

Holmes had many reasons to suspect that Jack was the poisoner. Why else would Mrs. Ferguson have struck him? She had probably been fighting to protect her baby. Jack had a motive to hate his stepmother and her son—they were stealing some of his father's love.

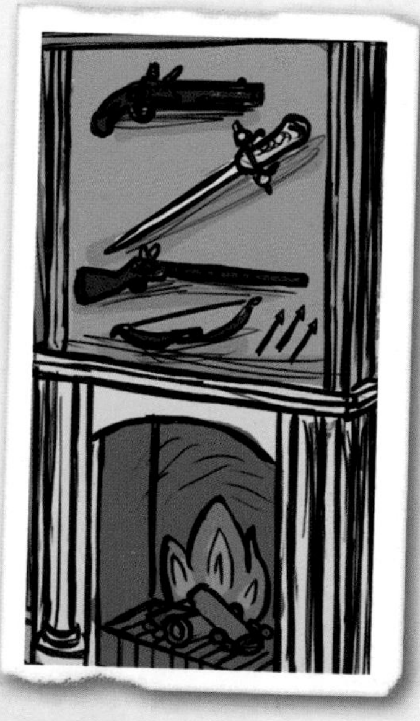

How did Holmes confirm his theory?

When Holmes arrived at the Fergusons' home, he had his answers. He saw poisoned arrow darts hanging on the wall. A scratch in the neck from one of those darts would kill the baby or cripple him for life. Holmes knew that the poisoner would have to test a dart to know if it worked. When Holmes saw that the dog, Carlo, was partly paralyzed, he knew that the poisoner had tested a dart on Carlo first.

How did Holmes confirm that Jack was the poisoner?

Holmes watched Jack as Robert Ferguson held his infant son. The hate and jealousy on Jack's face told Holmes all he needed to know. Jack was the poisoner, and there was no vampire. Holmes further confirmed his suspicions by questioning Mrs. Mason, who admitted that the danger to the baby had not passed. Camilla needed Mrs. Mason to protect the baby from Jack while she was locked in her room, so she trusted Mrs. Mason with her secret.

Further Reading and Websites

Donnelly, Jennifer. *A Northern Light*. San Diego: Harcourt, 2003.

Green, Mary. *Children Living in Victorian Britain*. Dunstable, UK: Folens Publishers, 2003.

Hoobler, Dorothy, and Thomas Hoobler. *The Ghost at Tokaido Inn*. New York: Penguin, 1999.

Jolley, Dan. *Vampire Hunt*. Minneapolis: Graphic Universe, 2008.

Krensky, Stephen. *Vampires*. Minneapolis: Lerner Publications Company, 2007.

Purslow, Frances. *Rugby*. New York: Weigl Publishers, 2006.

Remington, Gwen. *Life in Victorian England*. Farmington Hills, MI: Lucent Books, 2005.

Sherlock Holmes Museum
http://www.sherlock-holmes.co.uk

Souza, D. M., and Jack Harris. *Packed with Poison: Deadly Animal Defenses*. Minneapolis: Millbrook Press, 2006.

Tahan, Raya. *The Yanomami of South America*. Minneapolis: Lerner Publications Company, 2001.

221 Baker Street
http://221bakerstreet.org

About the Author

Sir Arthur Conan Doyle was born on May 22, 1859. He became a doctor in 1882. When this career did not prove successful, Doyle started writing stories. In addition to the popular Sherlock Holmes short stories and novels, Doyle also wrote historical novels, romances, and plays.

About the Adapters

Murray Shaw's lifelong passion for Sherlock Holmes began when he was a child. He was the author of the Match Wits with Sherlock Holmes series published in the 1990s. For decades, he was a popular speaker in public schools and libraries on the adventures of Holmes and Watson.

M. J. Cosson is the author of more than fifty books, both fiction and nonfiction, for children and young adults. She has long been a fan of mysteries and especially of the great detective, Sherlock Holmes. In fact, she has participated in the production of several Sherlock Holmes plays. A native of Iowa, Cosson lives in the Texas Hill Country with her husband, dogs, and cat.

About the Illustrator

French artist Sophie Rohrbach began her career after graduating in display design at the Chambre des Commerce. She went on to design displays in many top department stores including Galeries Lafayette. She also studied illustration at Emile Cohl school in Lyon, France, where she now lives with her daughter. Rohrbach has illustrated many children's books. She is passionate about the colors and patterns that she uses in her illustrations.